No Other Heart

by

Kay Winchester

Dales Large Print Books
Long Preston, North Yorkshire,
BD23 4ND, England.

British Library Cataloguing in Publication Data.

Winchester, Kay
    No other heart.

    A catalogue record of this book is
    available from the British Library

    ISBN   978-1-84262-865-2 pbk

First published in Great Britain in 1955 by Ward, Lock & Co Ltd.

Copyright © Kay Winchester 1955

Cover illustration © Stephen Carroll by arrangement with
Arcangel Images

The moral right of the author has been asserted

Published in Large Print 2012 by arrangement with
The Executor of Kay Winchester,
care of S. Walker Literary Agency

Dales Large Print is an imprint of Library Magna Books Ltd.

Printed and bound in Great Britain by
T.J. (International) Ltd., Cornwall, PL28 8RW

NO OTHER HEART

Excitement and glamour swayed Joanna Roberts, an orphan from a Scottish port, when she caught up with debonair and ruthless Garry Wetherall, and his background of London night life. Garry's appeal was much stronger and more dangerous than that of William Fenton and the correct atmosphere of his wealthy country home.

CHAPTER ONE

The headlamps picked her out. A solitary, unbelievable figure against the piled drifts of snow.

William Fenton slowed down a little more, and dipped the lights to warn her, but she didn't seem to notice.

She was slender, of medium height, clad in a coat with the collar turned up. Her hands appeared to be dug deep in her pockets, and a small bag was slung over one shoulder on a long strap. As she dragged each foot after the other, it came up out of the snow to reveal stockings soaked, and ordinary shoes that had chunks of snow clinging to them.

Pulling up beside her, William Fenton put a head out of the window, and asked: 'Would you like a lift? Filthy night!'

Her hair, dark and short and curly, like a boy's crop, had spangles of fresh snow in it. Her dark eyes were blazing with suspicion, and she shot her chin up at him.

'No, thanks!' she said grimly. 'I took one lift I had offered me to-night, but now I'm staying on these two legs of mine if it kills me!'

A smile twitched his mouth, but he said

good-humouredly enough, 'It probably will, you know. Those feet seem hardly well enough protected for this sort of weather. Any idea where you are?'

'I'm on the way to Beltonbridge,' she said shortly.

'I've just come from there,' he told her. 'It took me two hours in the car. You're going the wrong way.'

'The wrong way!' she repeated, and there was despair mingled with the disbelief in her voice. He decided that she was very tired and probably hadn't eaten anything for hours.

'Look here, hop in,' he urged. 'My place is just up there—'

She shook her head with determination. 'No, thanks,' she repeated, and started to walk on.

He shrugged a little, passed her with care, and made a skilful job of getting over the last few yards of slippery road up to the crossroads and the concealed turning that led sharply up the hill to Pevensey House.

At the crossroads, however, he hesitated again. If she ever got that far, she would assuredly get lost again, for snow completely obliterated the wings of the old-fashioned signpost, and she wasn't tall enough to reach up to them to clear them.

He backed, skirted the grass island which housed the signpost, and went back to her.

She had slipped and was picking herself up again. One leg was bleeding and she was examining it with fingers probably half-frozen.

'Don't be a silly chump,' he said sharply. 'Get in and I'll try to get you through to Beltonbridge. You needn't be afraid of me – I'm well known around here.'

She got in then, without a word, and slumped tiredly into the front seat. The snow on her shoes started to melt all over the floor of the car, but she didn't seem to notice. And then it started to snow again.

'How far is it to Beltonbridge?' she asked at last, breaking the silence with chattering teeth.

'About another five miles, as near as I can work it out. I can't even see just where we are.'

They had slowed down to a crawl, while he peered through the clogged windscreen to look for a tricky turning over a tiny bridge.

'No. I can't make it. We shall get stuck somewhere, and that will be the limit! I just about got through, coming from the town, with all those drifts, and it's not likely to get any better.'

'What are you going to do?' she asked sharply.

'I'm going to back out of here while the going's good,' he returned grimly, 'and I'm going to take you to my home. I'm sure my mother won't mind putting you up for the night.'

'I thought so! Funny business!' she exploded.

'Don't be an idiot. It's the least I can do. If you think I can have you on my conscience, wandering about on foot in this snowstorm, you'd better think again.'

There was a light in the porch of Pevensey House, which helped things a little, William Fenton thought irritably, as he skidded up the curving drive and pulled up with a screech of brakes.

Pevensey House loomed a great sprawling reddish-brown mass, topped with snow, against the white backcloth of bushes and trees. Silence lay over the place like a cloak, and the girl felt that the crunch of their feet must sound like fireworks in the still air. The door opened for them, and the brilliant shaft of light cut through the surrounding greyness and made her acutely aware of her cheap camel coat splattered with snow, and the too-bright stripy scarf she wore tucked into the throat. Her leg hurt where she had fallen, and it felt wet.

William Fenton experienced a wave of relief as his mother took the situation in her capable hands.

'William, my dear! How late you are!' she said, and kissed him. Then, turning her

8

attention to the girl, she said, 'But your leg is bleeding!'

William said hastily, 'This young lady got lost on the way to Beltonbridge. I tried to get her back, but the road's blocked.'

'I'm sorry,' the girl said. 'I wouldn't have caused any trouble for words, only I've got a job – the Copper Kettle in Beltonbridge – but I can't find my way about in England! No one knows where anywhere is!' and to the dismay of them all, she swayed slightly, and slid to the floor in an untidy little heap.

For a startled moment, mother and son looked at each other. Dismay rode undisguised over their faces.

'It must be Elaine!' Mrs Fenton whispered.

'It can't be,' William Fenton said uneasily, some time later, while he and his mother were waiting for Dr Lindsay to arrive.

'It must be,' his mother said firmly. 'But how came she to be lost? I've wondered and worried about the child all this week, but they are such an irresponsible family over there. She *did* say she came from Ireland, didn't she?'

'No,' he said, staring into the fire. 'She didn't say that her name was Elaine Sellers, either.'

'But what *did* she say, dear?'

'Very little, except that she didn't want me

9

to give her a lift. She thought she could walk into Beltonbridge and she was going in the wrong direction.'

His mother raised elegant eyebrows, but said nothing to that. Instead, she pursued her original trend of thought.

'Well, William, she did mention the Copper Kettle, and that seems to make everything clear. Elaine wanted to manage that place very badly. We know that from her letters. What she'll say when she finds that there isn't any Copper Kettle any more–'

'Don't fret about that, Mother. What's one teashop among all the property we own? We're lucky it didn't get burnt out before. I never did agree with wiring these ancient places. Odd about the girl, though. You say she's got a temperature?'

'A very high one. It was a good thing you managed to get her here when you did. She has a nasty cut on one leg, though. But what puzzles me is – she isn't like either Daniel or Margaret. You can usually see some likeness to a girl's father or mother, but there's nothing – nothing at all–'

'Mother, you haven't seen Daniel or Margaret for years and years. How can you possibly recall what they look like?'

'No, that's true. But then there's–' she began, and broke off, thinking of the girl's cheap clothes and handbag. Elaine would hardly be likely to dress like that. William didn't appear to have noticed that, but, she decided comfortably, men rarely noticed those little details.

She looked at her son, but abandoned the idea of telling him about it, as the doctor's arrival was announced.

The girl in the green guest-room lay very ill for four days, and then took a turn for the better.

'She's a very tough young woman, Dr Lindsay says,' Mrs Fenton remarked doubtfully, smiling a little at her son.

'Mother, if she really *is* Cousin Elaine–'

'Why, have *you* any doubts, dear?'

He looked thoughtfully at his cigarette. 'No, I suppose I haven't, really. Well, what are we going to do with her?'

'Oh, time enough to think about that later. What I must do, now that the telephone wires are repaired, is to dispatch a telegram to her parents, explaining briefly the situation. I don't suppose they were unduly anxious, but I think they ought to know that she hasn't been well.'

'Left it a bit late, Mother, for a telegram, didn't you, dear?'

'I left it until I could say she was recovering,' Mrs Fenton said, gently.

That meant, he knew, that his mother had been planning something.

'Now, Elaine, dear,' Mrs Fenton said, looking down at a pair of enormous dark brown eyes with tip-tilted lashes, 'I must talk to you. Dr Lindsay says you'll be up in a day or two, and I want you to know you're home.'

'Home?'

'Yes, dear. I'm your mother's cousin Mary. Isn't it amazing how you happened to be so near the end of your journey that night, and you didn't realize it?'

The girl frowned, and listened. Mary Fenton told her that she was to do nothing at all until she was really fit, and then they would see what she would like to do.

'But what about my job at the Copper Kettle?'

'I'm very sorry to say that that unfortunate teashop was burnt out the night before you came to us,' Mrs Fenton said.

The girl sat up in bed, but fell weakly back again.

'Don't worry, dear. The insurance will cover it, and probably William will have something new built on the site. He's a tiresome boy. He does like very old places so much, so perhaps he won't build something else. You'd probably like to work in another historic piece he'll pick up some time.'

'When will that be?'

'Oh, I can't really say. Are you so desperate to go out to work, then?'

'I have to eat,' she muttered, but Mary Fenton hardly heard it.

Dr Lindsay, who had been standing in the window, turned quietly.

'I'd like a word with our young lady, if I may,' he said firmly, and came and looked down at the girl.

Mary Fenton smiled. 'Get her well quickly. I've an idea that it's going to be very nice with someone of William's generation in the family. He's inclined to be very tiresome about company, but he'll have to be different with a young cousin around.'

Dr Lindsay watched her go out of the room, and then sat down by the bed.

'You're fit, practically,' he said. 'Still feeling a bit weak, though?'

She nodded. 'What's been the matter with me?'

He shrugged. 'When did you eat last?'

She turned her head away without answering.

'And you got soaked in the snow, *Joanna Roberts*.'

At the name, she swung round her curly cropped head on the pillow, and stared horrified up at him.

He nodded with satisfaction, and held up silently, for her inspection, a folded newspaper. Folded so that a photograph, her own, was visible for her to see. Underneath were a few lines, giving her name and description, and saying that the police wanted to get in touch with her, in connection with a jewel robbery.

She closed her eyes again. 'What are you going to do? Give me away?'

'That depends on you,' he said.

'How?' Her eyes were wary at once, and it struck him that she was wary and on the defensive more often than not.

'On whether you tell me the truth, about what the police want to see you about, and of course, what it is they do want to see you about.'

She moved restlessly, and finally turned to him.

'I haven't much choice, have I?'

'No,' he agreed.

She searched his face. He wasn't very old. Not a great deal older than William Fenton, whom she had put down to being about twenty-seven. But there was a shattering self-confidence about the doctor. He didn't exactly swagger, but gave you the impression that he would, if he didn't think it would look unprofessional. She decided that she didn't like him, but that wasn't strange. There hadn't been many men that she did like.

'It's all so silly,' she muttered angrily. 'So stupid. Such a waste. I was hungry. I usually am. I'd got fixed up for the Copper Kettle–'

'Oh, come now,' the doctor began, but she flared at him.

'It's true! There can be more than one job at the one place, can't there? I was taking a waitress's job. I don't know who this Elaine person is, they keep calling me, and I can't help it if she was going to work there as well. I'd got fixed up, and all I wanted was a meal, before I came to England—'

'There you go again,' the doctor warned her.

'I'm telling you the truth!' she said wildly. 'I never said I came from Ireland, did I? I came from Scotland, and I'd never been in England before. Just over the border, where everything's sane and simple.'

'Go on,' he said.

'Well, I got a lift down as far as Sunderland,' and she nodded, as his eyes involuntarily went to the newspaper account again. 'I just had enough money for a room for the night. In a boarding-house. One of the other boarders got talking to me and asked me out for a meal. How was I to know there was going to be anything more than just a meal?'

The doctor leaned back and considered her.

'I don't care if you believe me or not. I must have been seen about with him. That's all I know about it. After the meal he took me to the pictures and then back to the boarding-house. I never saw him again. I came south next day. I suppose the police think I'm a friend of his and know some-

15

thing about–'

'About what?' the doctor asked quietly.

'About what it says in the newspaper,' she retorted. 'I've seen that edition, too.'

'If what you say is true, then you should go to the police as soon as you're fit and tell them what you told me. It can't do any harm, if that's all that really happened.'

She shook her head fiercely.

'I'm not going to do anything about it.'

'Suppose I do something about it?'

Two pink spots came in her cheeks. 'It's your word against mine. I don't know why I told you so much. I wish I hadn't. But if you knew all I've been through since–'

'Since what? Haven't you any people of your own?'

She shook her head.

'You're quite on your own?'

She nodded. 'I've been kicking around since my grandfather died. I've managed, but I don't say it's been easy. But I've learned to fend for myself. First you have to be sure I'll be here when you bring the police back.'

He smiled. 'You won't get far on those weak legs at the moment, and where did you think you'd go, anyway? There's still snow around, you know.'

'What's it to you? What are you going to get out of it?' she asked him.

'It's my duty, since I know about it now.

Also, I won't have these nice people deceived. They think you're their relative, and you haven't said you're not.'

'I just wanted time,' she gasped. 'Have a bit of sense. D'you think I want to stop here, in *this* house? Just give me a chance to get out of here.'

'What's wrong with it?' he asked coolly. 'You know they're very rich, don't you? I imagine you think you've fallen on your feet.'

'That would be a rotten thing to say, if it wasn't so funny! You don't know me! This house is about as dull as–' she began, and then caught his sceptical expression. 'Don't look like that – I know! I got a glimpse of it when I came in, and I've seen the maids and Mrs Fenton. I want a bit of life. Just let me get out of here, that's all I ask!'

They eyed each other warily, and then the doctor suddenly smiled. 'All right, we'll see, then,' he said, getting up to go. 'You can get up to-day for a bit. All day to-morrow. I'll see you on Monday.'

Mrs Fenton had had the girl's clothes dried, but they hadn't been returned. Joanna fretted to get hold of someone to speak to, but no one came near her until the maid brought up an excellent lunch on a tray.

'See if you can find my things,' Joanna begged. 'I can get up for a bit, the doctor says.'

The maid smiled. She was elderly, and looked as if she would never be shaken out of that calm, correct manner.

'Madam says you're only to sit by the fire in a dressing-gown, miss,' she smiled, and went firmly out of the room.

Joanna devoured the soup, the breast of chicken, the pretty jelly, despite her misgivings about the silver tray and fine china. She thought about the doctor, and wondered what they had done with her clothes, and tried at last to get out of bed to see if there was a handy fire escape.

She felt curiously trapped, although she didn't think the doctor would do anything about her before he came again. It infuriated her that her legs were too weak to be stood upon, and it was while she was steadying herself by the bed, and wondering whose nightgown she was wearing, that Mrs Fenton came in.

'Well, dear, so you're trying to get up! That's splendid. Our good friend Dr Lindsay said you were to come down tomorrow, and that will be nice for William.'

She hesitated, and then said diffidently, 'I'm afraid your clothes got rather spoiled with your adventure in the snow. What happened to your luggage, my dear?'

Joanna climbed weakly back into bed and stared thoughtfully at the eiderdown. It was a strange frightening feeling, this weakness in the legs. She was tough, and had never been ill before. Never had to worry about what would happen to-day, to-morrow or the next day, because of her health. At some time or other, something had turned up. If she was hungry to-day, there would be a meal from somewhere or other to-morrow.

That was in the past. Now, this was England and strange territory, and at the same time her body had given her a warning that perhaps she had taken too many liberties in the past, run too many risks. It might not be so easy, having once caught a chill and been laid low.

'I don't know,' she said, thinking fast. For a fleeting second, she was strongly tempted to stay in this warm bed, eat this good food, and not to have to worry about plunging out into the cold and finding a job, and an indifferent room in someone's house, where there was shabbiness and a strong smell of greens cooking.

And then her old temper flared up. What business was it of anyone else's where her luggage was? What right had they to decide that her clothes were not fit to wear any longer? She had been out in worse weather than that snowstorm, and managed to tidy her clothes up again.

'Yes, I do!' she said, shooting up her chin. 'I just haven't got any luggage, and if you don't know your own cousin–'

Mary Fenton looked pained, and that made Joanna feel ashamed. She understood people shouting back at her, and had been brought up to believe that a good sparring match cleared the air. Mary Fenton, she perceived, would never shout, rarely let her anger or surprise show.

'I'm sorry. That was rude of me. Beastly, too. After you've been so kind and everything. But you *are* silly to take it for granted that I'm the person you expected.' She drew a deep breath, and took the plunge. 'I'm Joanna Roberts.'

She waited for the reaction, but none came. Then she recalled that the piece in the newspaper, and her photograph, seemed to have been limited to just that paper, and it was a popular one. Mrs Fenton probably didn't read that kind of newspaper. Her kind wouldn't be interested in girls who were the friends of house-breakers.

'I'd thumbed lifts all the way down from Scotland,' she added, waiting, but still nothing more from Mrs Fenton than that rather pained surprise.

'I'm just someone looking for a job, don't you see, not your cousin at all!'

'So, you're not Elaine,' Mrs Fenton murmured at last. 'That's rather a pity. I rather liked you, my dear.'

'Don't you like your cousin, then?'

'As you remind me,' Mary Fenton said,

with a smile, 'I haven't the least idea what she looks like. I have to find that out. Oh, I expect she'll be quite a nice young person, but you were–'

She didn't enlarge, but seemed satisfied, as if something that was bothering her had now been ironed out.

'Well, despite your somewhat unorthodox method of travelling, Joanna Roberts, I really can't let you have those clothes back. You must let me fix you up in–'

'What's wrong with my clothes?' Joanna asked fiercely.

Mary Fenton frowned, and didn't seem to hear. 'But you haven't a job now. You said you were going to work in our place–'

'As a waitress. Well, the Copper Kettle's gone, but there must be plenty of other places wanting waitresses. I'll be all right.'

'Oh, no. I feel we're responsible for you, somehow. You came such a long way to get this job. Where did you see it advertised?'

'A friend of mine sent me a cutting from a newspaper in London,' Joanna said, and a wave of hope lifted her, as she recalled that there was still Pixie Bellamy. Dear Pixie, who was never angry about anything, and who worked cheerfully in her aunt's boarding-house and didn't mind what she wore or what sort of work she did.

'Yes, I'll be all right,' Joanna said, nodding.

Mary Fenton looked at the pert little face

with its tanned skin, its full generous mouth, the large dark eyes and the winged eyebrows. There was something touching about Joanna, with her wild crop of dark curly brown hair, and her way of setting back her shoulders, as if she rather expected trouble, and got ready to take the shock of it.

'How old are you, my dear?'

'Twenty,' Joanna said. 'I can do any amount of things, so if one job falls through, there'll be another.'

'But it's winter-time, and you're a stranger here. How would you like a job with us here in this house?'

'What sort of job?' and again the wary look came into her eyes.

'Well, now, I just can't say for the moment. We have a large staff, and I could surely find you something useful to do, where I could keep an eye on you. I don't like the idea of a young thing like you having to fend for herself. It just doesn't seem right.'

'Oh, you mean make a job for me,' Joanna said, and felt a little thrill of disappointment. 'No. No, I couldn't have that. It's got to be a job anyone might get, so that I can walk out on it if I don't like something about it. That's me all over. Independent. I can't be nice like you. I'm sorry. I know how it sounds, but I must be free to do as I like, go as I like.'

'You'd be free here,' Mrs Fenton pressed.

'No. No, I wouldn't. I wouldn't like to walk out on you, because of your being so kind.'

There was a tap at the bedroom door.

The maid said Mr William wanted to speak to his mother urgently on the telephone, from his office.

Mrs Fenton sighed, and got up. 'I'll be back soon, dear,' she said, 'and I don't want you to attempt to get up until I return.'

William Fenton sounded rather anxious, at the other end of the line. 'Mother, about that girl, dear. We had our doubts, and–'

'Yes, dear, I know. She isn't Elaine.'

'Oh, you know?' He sounded relieved.

'Yes, she's just told me. What made you think of it, in the middle of your working morning?'

'Well, Elaine is here with me, in my office.'

Joanna came downstairs the next day. She had let Mrs Fenton over-ride her about her clothes. It wasn't difficult. As they lay on the brocaded chair by the bedside, Joanna realized what Mrs Fenton meant.

'Now, as my young cousin – or second cousin, rather – is coming down to lunch to-day, and as it's a Saturday and everyone expects to relax, why don't you slip into these things?' Mary Fenton persuaded. 'Surely nothing is more comfortable than a pleated skirt and this casual sweater?'

That was a mild way of putting it. Joanna cuddled into the soft cashmere jersey, with its clever neckline, and the silky scarf belonging to it, and noticed how the softly muted pattern combined the pale yellow of the woolly and the soft cinnamon brown of the skirt. She put them on, over her old undies; she had been adamant about that, but when she came to put on her shoes, there was really deadlock. Her shoes were completely ruined.

'You'd better put on this pair of little leather slip-ons,' Mary Fenton said calmly, 'and I'll send for some really nice shoes for you. You must let me do that for you; it will be in the nature of a little present. I'd like to, Joanna.'

Joanna's face slid into an engaging grin, as she brushed her tangled curls and tried not to look as she felt – very wobbly about the knees and tummy.

Mary Fenton said, 'Now, I'll show you around, or I'm afraid you'll get lost. This is a very confusing old house.'

Joanna scowled as they came out of the corridor from the bedrooms and looked down over a circular balcony on to the mosaic floor of a splendid hall. She had never been in a really large house before, and when she compared this with the last place in which she had slept, she reddened angrily.

'It's period, you know,' Mrs Fenton's soft

24

voice told her. 'My son loves historic backgrounds. You must ask him to show you his collection of photographs of the properties he's bought recently.'

They went down a wide curving staircase, which reminded Joanna a little of a staircase she had once seen in a private museum and then they were in the library, a forbidding room gloomy with dark panelling and the rich hues of rows and rows of old books. The dogs sprawled on the rug looked unfriendly, and after Mrs Fenton left her, and closed the door on her, Joanna edged clear of the circle round the fire and stood uneasily at the far side of the room.

Presently the door opened and a very lovely girl came carelessly into the room, speaking over her shoulder to the servant. She spoke to the dogs, and warmed her hands at the fire. Joanna noticed that although she didn't tell them to, the dogs moved out of her way.

'Hallo!' the girl said, suddenly catching sight of Joanna. 'Who are you? I haven't seen you before! New secretary or something?'

Joanna flushed. 'I'm a guest here,' she said, defiantly.

'You don't act like a guest, hanging about up that end. Why don't you come and get a warm near the fire?'

Joanna fancied one of the dogs lifted the side of its mouth, making a preliminary

25

soundless snarl.

The girl noticed, and laughed. 'Oh, scared of dogs! They won't hurt you. Clear out, Kim. Be a gentleman.'

The dog got up and slunk away, and the girl said, 'Oh, well, if you're a guest, we'd better introduce ourselves. I'm Lavinia Durrance.'

Mrs Fenton came in then, with another girl, and behind her, William Fenton.

'Oh, I'm so glad you two have met,' she said. 'Now, Lavinia, I want you to know my young cousin from Ireland. Elaine Sellers. Poor Elaine had such a trying crossing that she couldn't face the journey south. So she found the home of an old school-friend in Cheshire, and wisely stayed there until the weather was less inclement.'

Elaine and Lavinia promptly plunged into an animated account of the crossing, how many times they had made it, how it compared with the Channel crossings; Paris and the latest shows in London.

William Fenton passed cigarettes around, but Joanna shook her head. 'I don't smoke,' she said.

He sat back and lit a pipe, and listened for a moment to his gentle mother trying to turn the conversation back so that Joanna could be included.

'Joanna comes from Scotland, don't you, dear?'

'Oh, which part?' Lavinia wanted to know. 'My people come from Strathglennie.'

'Rorton. Just over the border,' Joanna said, in a small voice.

'Oh, but that's a port or something, isn't it?' Lavinia asked, wrinkling her nose.

'New town, I thought,' Elaine offered, shrugging, and they switched the conversation to building houses, and what Lavinia's family's London house was like.

William said quietly, 'I haven't seen you to speak to, have I? Are you better now?'

Joanna said, 'I'm quite well now, and I want to get away.'

'Where will you be going?'

Joanna could feel that the other two girls were half-listening, despite the conversation they were keeping up which automatically shut her out.

She looked at William and saw that he was sincere in wanting to know. Like his mother, he wanted to help her, without patronizing, without anything but kindness.

He was a very good-looking young man, and because he didn't seem to be aware of just how good-looking he was, he made Joanna uneasy. Like his kindness, his naturalness was a thing unknown to her. She understood the cattiness of the two girls. She had met that sort of thing before, but she hadn't met anyone like William Fenton or his mother before, and when she didn't understand a thing, her instinct was to get away from it.

'Oh, London. I've got friends there. I'll get fixed up with something.'

Her off-hand manner surprised him. He looked across at his mother, and caught her shaking her head at him, as if, she, too, had encountered the same brusqueness. He decided that Joanna was feeling pretty low and out of it, so he decided to leave her alone for a while.

They lunched in the dining-room, another gloomy panelled room with a magnificent sideboard. There were bowls of flowers down the centre of the long table, and there wasn't a tablecloth. Just little mats, and the gleaming reflections of silver and cut glass in the polished wood surface, and later, when the lights were put on because the day was so dark and cheerless, they too, reflected themselves into the table-top. Joanna thought of fish and chips in a hot steamy little café she knew and liked, and she felt homesick. It had been fun when grandfather was alive. He had been a seaman, and told her about all the foreign ports he had known in his turbulent youth. She wished she could have been a boy, and got about and really done things.

The dreadful day wore on. Lavinia went home because her family had friends coming to dinner. She was, it appeared, the daughter of a near neighbour. Elaine was staying in the house and monopolized William. She had beautifully cut light brown hair which looked like the hair you saw on models in hairdressers' windows.

Joanna was acutely conscious of the rough look of her own curly pate, and kept trying to smooth it down. When Elaine and William settled down to spend the evening with gramophone records, Joanna could hardly keep her eyes open. Classical music of the heavier type meant nothing to her, and the whole business struck her as being more dreary than she had envisaged it when she spoke to the doctor.

Mrs Fenton said kindly, 'Perhaps you'd like your supper on a tray in your room, dear. You mustn't stay up too long the first day.'

Joanna gratefully escaped, with the book which William Fenton had offered her. It was a thriller, but she discarded it after the first chapter. It was about a girl who had been out with a man she hardly knew, and he turned out to be a jewel thief, and they were both on the run from the police.

Somehow she got through Sunday, which was a little better because other people came in. There was a bishop and a scientist, who both spoke tenderly to her, as if she were an attractive puppy. They got the impression that she, too, was a distant relative, and William and his mother did nothing to disillusion them. Joanna chafed under their kindness, but comforted herself with the thought that people like this were hardly likely to have seen her picture in the popular newspapers.

She was almost herself again now. The weakness had left her legs. The good food and the comfort of her bed, and the quiet, all helped her to make rapid strides to recovery. But on Sunday night, sleep wouldn't come. The doctor would be calling the next day, and she wasn't sure what was going to happen.

Restless, she decided to go downstairs and hunt about in that dreadful library for something she might be able to read. She recalled that the dogs were shut up somewhere outside at night, and so she had nothing to fear.

The house was a chilling place in the darkness, but from old habit, Joanna took the pocket torch out of her handbag and found her way after two or three false starts.

She couldn't find the light-switch. There were several sets of lights in the great ceiling, and the switchboard at the door was too complicated to risk putting on the wrong one, so she wandered all round the shelves, putting her little torchlight on the names of the books. She was again at the far end of the room when the lights all came on.

She swung round gasping, but it was only William Fenton, almost fully dressed, with a silk dressing-gown on. He looked more attractive than in his week-end tweeds, and he was smiling and faintly puzzled.

'What the deuce are *you* doing here?' he asked softly, closing the door behind him, and putting off some of the lights. 'We don't want to disturb the rest of the house,' he smiled.

'I'm sorry,' she muttered. 'I can't sleep, and I don't like the book your mother gave me.'

He strolled over to her and looked down at her. 'What's wrong, Joanna? What's wrong with you, to make you like this?'

'What d'you mean?' she demanded.

'There you are, you see! Always on the defensive. Hasn't life treated you very well?'

'Does it, ever?' she countered fiercely. 'I wouldn't like to be you – living in this awful place, with awful people visiting you. I'd go crazy if I had to live here.'

'Pretty dull, isn't it?' he agreed.

'D'you mean that?' she gasped.

He nodded, still smiling. 'It's one of the penalties of being very rich. One has to live to a pattern.'

'You're laughing at me!'

'No, indeed I'm not. You'd be surprised if you knew the things I'd really like to do, instead of driving to and from town every day, and making all my money and property work. There isn't much fun in it.'

She hunched a shoulder. 'At least you're never hungry and you don't wonder where you're going to sleep next.'

'You shouldn't have to do that, either,' he told her. 'How long have you been alone?'

'On and off, since I was nine. Grandfather gave a loose eye to me. You don't know what that means, do you? I suppose you had a nannie and dozens of servants to look after you! I had just my grandfather (when he was at home) and when he wasn't, I knocked about on my own, and cadged a meal off neighbours.'

'Poor little devil,' he murmured.

'Don't be sorry for me!' she flashed. 'I'm tough. I can take anything. Oh, just this once, I was a fool. Or unlucky. I don't know. You see—'

She searched his face, decided that Dr Lindsay had told him nothing about the police wanting her, and weighed in the balance whether, in the interests of truth, it was worth losing a possible friend. 'Never close all the doors, lass,' her grandfather had said. 'Never make up your mind that you'll not need this or that, any more, whether it's clothes or people. You don't know. If you chuck away something, ten chances to one you'll need it, some day, and you'll wish you hadn't been so keen on cutting loose.'

'I lost my luggage,' she improvised, searching his eyes once again, to see how that sounded. Of what use telling him frankly that having discovered the disquieting truth about Slim Halloway, who'd taken her out for the evening, she'd decided to cut and run, without going back to her digs for her luggage. A passing lorry, and escape from awkward questions. All her life she had had to have a get-away. Fear of being held against her will amounted almost to a phobia with her.

'If I hadn't been without it, I'd have had boots on, and I wouldn't have caught a chill. I never have, before. I've slept out of doors before this,' she said proudly, and then could have bitten out her tongue. Women of his world didn't do that.

He smiled. 'Good show. So have I. In the army, with my men. It's good to learn to rough it. Now, Joanna, tell me – what do you want of life?'

'Want?' She was puzzled. Money meant nothing to her. Clothes were things to play with, like toys, but hampered one with getting about. Without tasting good things, she had no particular desire for them.

'What's your ambition? I might be able to put you in the way of a really good job, if I only knew what you were after. I have so many contacts, you see. What are you good at?'

'Oh, work! I take what I can. It doesn't matter. I like to be free, though. I want to get about and see places.'

'Do you speak any foreign languages?'

He was thinking aloud, but she took it the wrong way. 'Oh, yes, seven or eight,' she said sarcastically, 'having been to college and all that. Are you being funny?'

He was at once contrite. 'I just wondered if your grandfather had picked up any, and taught you. These old seamen can get about pretty well, I know,' he said, at once. 'I wish I could think of something. If you were only–'

He broke off, smiling.

'Only what?' she demanded.

'A little more tractable,' he said chuckling. 'I might fix you up as a companion-secretary, to travel all over the place, but frankly, I can't see you dancing attendance on any of my mother's old friends.'

She saw the funny side of that, and her face immediately broke into that enchanting grin which his mother had seen and liked. Soon she was laughing, and he found she had that haunting kind of laughter that is utterly infectious in its gaiety and love of life. He was laughing too, his own quiet, amused laughter, when the door was flung open and Elaine stood there.

They sprang round, guiltily, their laughter broken off in mid-air, as she said, tartly,

'Can anyone join the party, or is it a private one?'

Her light brown hair still looked impeccable. She had on a glamorous dressing-gown of palest pink velvet which at once reminded Joanna of siren-type film stars she had seen in films at the little picture-house round the corner.

Elaine, in that moment, became established in Joanna's mind as the beautiful enemy, the lovely creature who would, throughout the length of the film to the very end, fool the hero into thinking she was the one woman for him. With all her usual energy, Joanna promptly hated Elaine, and glared stormily at her across the length of the library.

William said easily, 'Joanna wants a book. I heard a noise and came down and found her. Let's get you something readable while we're here,' he said, turning to Joanna.

'Yes, let's,' Elaine said nastily, putting on more lights, and preparing to stay and help.

'Never mind,' Joanna said. 'I've lost the urge to read. Good night,' and she strode past Elaine and ran up the stairs.

William watched her go, thoughtfully, and then he turned to Elaine. 'What made you come down, Elaine? Can't you sleep?'

'I heard someone go past my door. And then I heard people talking and laughing,' she said shortly.

'Oh, I see,' he smiled, and in the lift of her eyebrows, he saw at once the likeness to her mother, whom he had met as a boy. He went upstairs smiling to himself. So they could now be sure that they had the right person, in Elaine. She was undoubtedly his cousin. He found himself wishing, a little wistfully, that Joanna Roberts could have been his cousin instead.

It was after tossing and turning for three hours, that Joanna finally got up, routed out her old clothes she had come in, and decided to leave Pevensey House before anyone was about.

It was a combination of the presence of Elaine, and the probing goodness of William Fenton which decided her, rather than the looming visit of the doctor and his menacing shadow, the next day. William Fenton was sorry for her, she knew, and although he was sorry for her in a way which she couldn't possibly resent, nevertheless, it would drive him to fix her up in something before very long. She didn't want to be fixed up by anyone, least of all by that very nice young man. She must kick for herself, she told herself fiercely.

She tried to write a note, on the back of an envelope she found in her bag, but words didn't come easily, and finally she abandoned the task, and just left. She had to break a pantry window to get out, because she couldn't manipulate the bolts on the great door of the hall, and she was afraid of waking the dogs. She had, too, to 'borrow' a pair of rubber boots from the garden room, because she had nothing for outdoors. She was sorry about that, but didn't think they'd be missed. It couldn't be helped, anyway. Having found the high-road, and a passing lorry, the rest was easy. She sat back, and gulped in deep breaths of the icy night air, and felt free.

She reached London at six o'clock, and took a trolley bus to Cedars Street. She knew how to get to Pixie's house, from the often repeated instructions in Pixie's letters.

There was slush everywhere. Only the roofs had white snow left in the crevasses, and in the shadows of the chimney stacks where the fitful wintry sunshine hadn't reached. Joanna sniffed at the familiar air and felt at home. Not because she had ever been in London before, but because she was a product of the town. This might well be the port, where she had been born and bred, except that the docks were too far away to be heard or seen.

Cedars Street was a long, long road of faded Victorian terrace houses. Iron railings, with a dreary laurel in the sooty soil of the front garden, were common to each house, and finished the grey picture. For the rest, there was a quantity of greyness that would have disheartened anyone else. But to Joanna, this was the type of thing that spelt home. Rows on serried rows of straight windows, greyish lace curtains behind them, grey bricks and grey stone steps upwards to dim front doors and downwards to shallow areas; rows and rows of little smoky chimneys on stunted stacks, and grey slate roofs.

She started whistling softly under her breath, and hitched her shoulder bag further back. She saw a newsboy settle himself on an upturned box on the corner of the street, and after a second's hesitation, she bought an early edition. A small piece of news on the third page, set her walking on air. All her troubles were over. The police, in that distant Northern town, had located Slim Halloway, and had lost all interest in anyone else. She was no longer wanted for questioning. They had found the criminal. She was really free.

She found number twenty-nine, scuttered down the area steps, and banged noisily at the door. Pixie's letters, lengthy and scrawled over pale pink notepaper without any lines, had given her the set-up of this house, and she knew that Pixie would be the only one about yet.

The door was opened a cautious couple of inches, through which a near-Persian, also pale grey, came out with a rush. Then Pixie herself, blonde hair still in curlers, appeared.

After mutual stares, the two girls burst into delighted laughter. 'Ow! It's *you!* Why didn't you say you were coming? How *are* you?' Pixie shouted, pulling Joanna inside. 'Now don't stand there letting all the cold in. Come inside and have a cup of something hot. What a time to turn up! D'you know what the time is? Here, I like your fancy footwear!'

Joanna grinned down at the gumboots, several sizes too large for her, and plunged into an account of all that had happened to her since she left her home town.

'Have a cupper,' Pixie said, thrusting a cup of steaming sweet tea into Joanna's hands, her eyes never leaving Joanna's face. When she had inspected the newspaper, she nodded.

'I saw the picture of you. Said to myself, hallo, hallo, hallo, what's going on here. Didn't seem right, somehow. Oh, I know you're one for a lark, and all that, but you always had your head screwed on the right way. Oh, well, you never can tell how people are going to turn out, can you?'

They stared at each other, and then Pixie said, slowly, 'When I was up in Rorton, your granddad was alive.'

Joanna nodded, and bit her lip. She still

felt his loss very keenly.

'Ever wish you'd come back with me then?' Pixie went on. 'You could have lived here with us and got a job, and you wouldn't have noticed being left alone, so much.'

'He was old and ill and tired. I couldn't leave him,' Joanna said. 'Got a room for me now, Pixie?'

'Of course. I don't have to say so, do I? Well, that's to say, it isn't much of a room, but it will be all to yourself. Up at the top, next to mine. You could work here too, if you wanted. Aunt could do with extra help. Doesn't pay much, but it'd be company for me, and there's plenty of fun going. All the lodgers are young and not so hard-up as you'd think.'

'Rule No. 1. Never work for friends,' Joanna grinned, and they both roared with delighted laughter.

'You and your rules,' Pixie chuckled, suddenly remembering the curlers and feverishly undoing them as masculine footsteps were heard on the basement stairs.

Joanna peeled off her topcoat and kicked the gumboots off. Her jersey was scarlet, and in the glow of the open front of the stove, she was a warm and vital thing, her great dark eyes dancing and her hair – damp from the night mists – curling tightly to her head. The newcomer stood in the doorway, leaning easily against the lintel.

'Hallo, there! What have we got here?' he said, in a slow drawling voice that had a mixture of insolence and caressing in it.

'Oh, it's you, Mr Wetherall,' Pixie said briskly. 'Now didn't I tell you yesterday that guests aren't allowed in the basement? It's the only bit of the house that's ours, and we want to keep it to ourselves.'

'And so you shall,' Garry Wetherall said mockingly, bowing from the waist. 'If you'll be so kind as to send your other visitor packing upstairs with me. I could do with a bit of company in the dining-room. It's as chilly as a tomb and just about as lively.'

Pixie smothered a retort and thought quickly. 'Here, don't let my aunt know, but I'll give you a hot cupper if you'll clear off afterwards. Here, Jo, pour it out for him, there's a dear, while I set things to rights.'

She bustled off to the big scullery, where they could hear her banging pots and frying pans about, and shovelling coal as if ten devils were after her. Joanna poured another cup of tea, and handed it to Garry Wetherall.

'Cat got your tongue?' he murmured.

'No. Mother said I'm not to talk to strangers,' Joanna told him, pertly, and turned her back on him, warming her hands at the stove. The warmth was good, and she wriggled her toes in her mud-spattered stockings.

41

He looked at her feet, at the torn stocking, the blood and the mud. His glance travelled up her old black skirt, and her scarlet wool jersey which clung closely to the nice lines of her lithe young figure. His eyes lingered on hers, did a lightning leap over her hair in a way that made her feel he had caressed it, and then back to her eyes again.

'That's the girl! Smart with the comeback. That's the way I like 'em. Mother says I'm not to be alone. It's bad for my nerves. How about it?'

'How about what?'

They heard Pixie coming back.

He said quickly, 'Relation or boarder?'

'Friend of the family,' Joanna shrugged. 'What's it to you?'

'Know London?' he grinned, and she reddened, realizing that he had picked up the faint burr, which had puzzled the Fenton family, and might easily have been either Irish or in fact north of the border. She had done her best to iron it out, but it still caught her unawares sometimes.

'You know I don't,' she fumed.

'Get yourself fixed up, and I'll put that right,' he grinned, 'to-night.'

Pixie scowled as he bowed himself out. 'Don't listen to him,' she said, as a general warning.

'If you mean that, why did you clear out like that?' Joanna returned, and both girls shouted with that old easy laughter that they had shared so often, in the years when Pixie had been working in Rorton, and living next door to Joanna.

'Dated?' Pixie asked delicately.

'He thinks so,' Joanna chuckled. And then, serious again, she said urgently, 'Pixie, I've got to get a job. Got a newspaper? The sort with ads in? This one hasn't got any.'

'The shop round the corner's got cards in the window,' Pixie said easily. 'If you must go out in this weather, that is.'

'Must,' Joanna assured her.

Joanna's luck was in, and she had got herself a new job before she met Pixie's aunt. Mrs Adey was a tall, sad-looking woman, whose thin despairing voice disguised the iron rule she held over number twenty-nine. She moved about slowly, and rarely seemed to look at anyone, but she missed nothing.

'Staying?' she asked Joanna, without much interest.

'If I may,' Joanna grinned. 'I've got a job at The Orange Tree – waitress.'

'Oh, well. Watch your tips,' Mrs Adey said. 'Best get some clothes. Pixie'll help you.'

'I've got just the thing for you to-night,' Pixie said, with enthusiasm, after they had washed up the boarders' dinner things and had their own meal. 'I'll lend you anything you want, until you can look round and buy some. Just say the word, and I'll lend the

43

cash, and you can pay me off as you get it.'

Joanna said briefly, 'Thanks,' and stared at Pixie. There was a warmth and security in this house, despite the brevity of Pixie and her aunt. Joanna had never found it easy to voice her thanks either, but Pixie understood the long look and all it meant. She patted Joanna's hand.

'Come and see the things, kid.'

They pelted up the stairs to the top of the house, into Pixie's own room, which had been made comfortable in a way to suit the owner's taste. The dregs of the house's furniture had found its way up here, and Pixie had put frilly petticoats on everything (even the rails of the old iron bedstead) and blue bows. There were a lot of lights on the dressing-table, fixed from the central light by one of Pixie's men-friends who had been an electrician.

Pixie flung open the enormous wardrobe and routed among the things, and found a three-quarter violet silk skirt, very full, and trimmed with a wide braid border. There was a pale lilac jersey with a high neck, and sequins sewn all over it, and a short fur-cloth jacket. 'And get into these nylons, for heaven's sake, and these sandals. Oh, never mind the slush, he's got a car of sorts. You'll have a good time.'

'How d'you know I will?' Joanna wanted to know.

'He tried me out, the first night he was here.'

'And–?' Joanna prompted.

'And I found his pace too quick for my idea of leisure,' Pixie, who was on her feet all day, retorted, with feeling. 'He's a fine dancer, I'll hand him that. But he doesn't know what bedtime means. You'll be lucky if you're in by three. Best take a key.'

Joanna found Garry Wetherall waiting in the hall. 'Buck up, girl, the old bus'll freeze up on us if I keep her waiting much longer. Here, let's have a look at you. Not bad – not bad at all.'

Joanna tied the blue scarf Pixie had lent her, round her hair, and dug her hands into the jacket pockets. The sandals were flat-heeled and comfortable, and the nylons felt good. She had a job, and someone to spend the first evening in London with. She had a home with Pixie and her aunt. The police had lost interest in her. She wasn't on her own any more.

She went down the steep front steps and followed Garry Wetherall into his car, a shabby saloon which had a remarkably good performance, whatever its exterior looked like.

William Fenton and his mother seemed far away, as she and Garry ate at a little Chinese restaurant, and went on in the car to an underground club to dance.

'We're perfect, together,' Garry said suddenly, in a short, surprised voice.

'Anyone'd dance perfectly with you,' Joanna retorted.

'I didn't say perfect at dancing,' he said. 'I meant everything.'

She raised startled brown eyes to his. 'Listen, Garry Wetherall, we only met this morning,' she reminded him.

'I know girls, honey,' he said grimly. 'Once in a life-time this happens. You meet. Click, something falls into place. You *know*, way inside you, that you've met the *one*.'

She batted her eyelids in a way she had when she was frightened. Their limbs still moved together, in perfect unison, over the dance floor, but their eyes were filled with different emotions. His grey ones, keen, devil-may-care, were filled with a new excitement. But fear was the only emotion she felt. A trapped feeling again. Someone was trying to box her in. Settle things for her. She fought like a startled animal.

'How can you *know?*' she retorted, softly jeering.

'I do,' he said roughly. 'We're made for each other. Don't smile. D'you think I like it, either? Don't let anything get stale, that's my motto. But you and I... We'll have fun together, I know that. We'll fight together, maybe. You're tough, and so am I. But I'll tell you this. I feel it in my bones. Maybe we

46

won't finish up together, but if we ever split up, it'll never be the same with anyone else. Spoilt, because there'll be nothing like this again.'

She shivered. The excitement had died out of his eyes, and he stared morosely over her head. He, too, she divined, didn't like being held down. She suddenly remembered William Fenton, and the gentle smile in his eyes as he looked down at her, in the great library of his home. 'Poor little devil,' he had said, and there had been infinite tenderness in his voice at that moment. Now that she had left him behind, in a past that would never come back, she felt a little lost. Had that been security? What was this, this wild excitement, tinged with the frightening closing-in, which she felt now?

She looked up searchingly, and found Garry's eyes on her. His arm tightened round her.

'Chin up, kid,' he said, and a smile spread all over that tanned, ruthless face of his. 'We don't know what's in store for us, but we'll extract the last ounce of fun while it lasts.'

CHAPTER TWO

Pixie didn't like what she heard about that first evening.

'Like I said, kid, watch out. Where else did he take you? What time did you get in, anyway?'

Joanna frowned. 'About two. We went dancing at another place after that. I don't know where it was. He just bundled me into the car and drove round a lot of back streets.'

Pixie nodded. 'He's all right, of course, but it's his pace I don't like. See, I don't suppose he meant all that blah about you both being made for each other. What I want to make sure is that you know that his type talk big like that. Don't let him take you for a ride, kid, if you see what I mean!'

Joanna nodded without rancour. Pixie had often given her advice in the past. She was four years older, and it was tacitly agreed between them that she knew her way about, and that anything she had to impart in the way of experience, was to be snapped up by the younger girl.

'Just the same, Pixie,' Joanna said slowly, 'there's something about him that, oh, I don't know. No one else has ever made me feel like this. I don't know,' she said again, shrugging, as if to throw off any effect that Garry Wetherall may have left on her. 'I don't like to feel like this about anyone.'

'Like what?' Pixie asked warily.

'Well, it's all sort of mixed. I'm scared and want to back out, but at the same time I want to find out more about it all, I want to go on, just to see if what he said came true.'

'Here, don't talk like that!' Pixie exclaimed, unwinding a curler and replacing it carefully, taking in the strand of hair that had worked out, and lay straightly on her cheek. ('Wish I could afford a perm,' she muttered). 'No, don't talk like that, it's tempting fate, that's what it is. If I were you, I'd have a good look round, and find someone else. Someone who didn't get you excited and then spoil it by giving you the creeps.'

'Is that what your boy-friend's like?' Joanna wanted to know.

Pixie nodded. 'He's all right,' she conceded. 'Just what I wanted. Steady. I know what to expect. A night or two at the flicks, with a dance flung in once a week. Little presents now and again, and no strings. Yes, Alec's all right. I can't complain.'

Joanna hunched a shoulder, and curled up her knees, as she settled herself more comfortably on the side of Pixie's bed. Not looking directly at her friend, but rather looking over at her reflection in one of the many faded mirrors, she said, slowly,

'That isn't what I want.'

'Let's have it,' Pixie commanded. 'What *do* you want, and then we'll know what to expect if you don't turn up at all one night.'

'Oh, nothing like that! No, what I want is someone *different.*'

'No such thing,' Pixie said hardily. 'All men are alike. They just pretend to be different.'

Joanna shook her head and thought about William Fenton. In Pixie's book of rules, no man, however rich and important, stood half-dressed in his own library in the small hours, talking about jobs and life to a strange girl, who was almost completely undressed. Pixie would put a far different interpretation on that little scene if Joanna were foolish enough to tell her about it, but this had been one of the incidents she had omitted to mention. She found she was rather diffident about telling Pixie too much about William Fenton.

'Now what are you dreaming about?' Pixie wanted to know.

'A man who'll fall in love with me and marry me and still be in love with me for all my life,' Joanna said firmly.

Pixie's jaw dropped, and then she started to laugh. 'No, that isn't possible,' she said. Turning serious, she went on, 'See here, kid, you don't have to be silly and believe all you read about and see at the pictures. In life, it's either love – with nothing secure – or marriage, and, well, you know what that means. Look at Auntie, left with a boarding-house on her hands. Whether you lose 'em or keep 'em, a man expects one thing. He needs waiting on for the rest of his life, and his wife is just the one who does it, and stands over the stove and the wash-tub all the hours of the day *and* night. And if she gets a treat now and then, she'll be lucky.'

'What are you courting for, then, if that's what it's like?' Joanna demanded.

Pixie lay back with her arms behind her head and stared at the ceiling. Her face was a smeared mask of thick white cream, and her lashes, their natural colour at bedtime, looked sickly pale and made her eyes look a lighter blue. 'Habit,' she said, succinctly.

Joanna waited.

'See, Jo, if you don't court someone, then you get nothing. Either way, a woman has to work and cook and wash. But if you have your fun courting (and make it last as long as you can, without losing him, of course), then when you get a place and respon-sibilities of your own, you've got something to look back on. It's about all you get,' she finished, philosophically.

'What will I get from Garry Wetherall?'

Pixie looked sharply at her.

51

'Precious little, I'd say.'

'What did you want to fix me up with him for?'

'Now, listen, Jo, who fixed who up?' Pixie reasoned. 'I saw you were wanting to go out with him. No sense in my trying to stop it. The least I could do was to find you some glad rags. Besides, you were half-way there, anyway.'

The evenings with Garry raced by all too quickly.

'Come swimming,' he commanded, one Monday. 'It's a dead duck night. Nothing worth seeing anywhere. We'll run out to a roadhouse I know, where there's a covered pool.'

'It's winter,' Joanna reminded him, laughing.

'Like I said. A covered pool, heated. Well, warmed, anyway. Come on, or don't you swim?'

'Of course I swim, but I don't happen to have a swimsuit yet. Give me a week and I'll get one.'

'I've got one – just right for you.'

'No!' she said quickly.

'Don't tell me you wouldn't take a present from me,' he said, leaning over her a little, and grinning that impudent grin of his.

'No man ever bought me things to wear,' she retorted.

'What, never a necklace or ear-rings?' he asked.

'That's different,' she flashed.

He shook with quiet laughter, and took a parcel out of his pocket. A small package, in which was folded with expert hands a model swim-suit, Old Gold satin with gilt dragons all over it.

She drew in her breath, and shook her head fiercely.

'I couldn't take such an expensive present.'

'Not even for Christmas?'

'Christmas isn't here yet,' she retorted.

'A matter of three weeks,' he reminded her, taking one of her hands, and draping the lovely thing over it. 'As to that, I got it at cost price. A mere nothing. One of the many tasty lines my firm does, in a small way.'

'Just what does your firm do, Garry?'

'Little girls shouldn't ask questions. You don't understand the commercial world, anyway.'

As she still hesitated, he jeered: 'Go on, we know you're a good girl. Take the thing and get a bit of fun out of life, for once. All I'm asking you to do is swim in it!'

She coloured, and decided to go. But she didn't show the swimsuit to Pixie. Somehow she didn't want Pixie's shrewd comments to-night. She was tired, and her feet hadn't got acclimatized to the long hours and the running about, which her present job demanded. She had worked before in small teashops, where the business was patchy, and in the quiet periods during the day the waitresses had a chance to get off their feet. In her present job they were busy at all hours.

The roadhouse was gay with lights, and there were a lot of long, new cars parked outside. Some of the people had evening dress, others were dressed casually like themselves. Joanna, in a new black skirt, very full, and a plain black jersey, with an imitation pearl necklace, felt better dressed than she had on the evening of her first dance with Garry.

She felt his eyes on her, and was surprised when he said, sharply: 'You want red. Rich, glowing red and honey-gold. Not black!'

'When my ship comes home, I'll see what I can do for you,' she said lightly.

'How about letting me?' he murmured in her ear, as he swung her to her feet and started to dance.

'I thought we were going to swim?' she muttered, trying to pull away from the exciting nearness of his body. He was a big young man, with a splendid physique and an animal grace, and although his clothes were casual in the extreme, he always seemed just right, wherever he was.

'Later,' he said, with finality. 'Let yourself go, Joanna, you're stiff and pulling away from me.'

'Mother said I wasn't to dance like this with strange young men.'

'I don't believe you ever had a mother,' he said coolly, as he fixed her eyes with his own. 'I believe you got all this advice from misguided reading. You follow your instincts, and you won't go far wrong, my child.'

A little flutter of fear chased through her. If she followed her instincts, she reasoned, she would be pressing close to him, succumbing to the wild emotions that often threatened to engulf her, when she was with him.

She closed her eyes and danced, and so missed the little half-tender smile of satisfaction that lingered for a moment round Garry's mouth.

The pool was a luxury one, round with a domed roof and central heating. Blue tiles lining the pool made the water seem to be that colour. People sat about around the edges, showing off swimsuits no more lovely than her own.

Joanna didn't dawdle, but went straight away to the high diving platform, and did a clean swallow dive. Garry followed, and at once they made a little star performance of their own, as if oblivious of everyone else around them. Garry shallow-dived, holding her hand, taking her beneath the waters with him; and catching the spirit of the thing, Joanna weaved in and out, making leg and arm patterns with him, and coming up with him, laughing, and shaking the water out of her tight curls. The new swimsuit fitted her like a sheath, and in the blue pool she looked like an exotic flower, with her brown skin and dark hair and lashes, and the glow of health in her cheeks.

There was a faint burst of applause from some of the onlookers as they came out, and someone said that they must be professionals.

Joanna, embarrassed, pulled away from Garry and ran away and got changed quickly. Her tiredness was gone, and she felt all aglow, but there was uneasiness, too. She didn't like people to watch her when she was playing. Any suggestion of exhibitionism was distasteful to her.

'Don't be a fool,' she cautioned herself. 'There might be something in it. Someone important might see you, put you in an under-water show or something.'

But it was no good scolding herself. She still didn't like the idea, and didn't care much if she did miss any chances.

Garry, however, thought differently. He said at once, 'Let's get out of here,' and when they were in the car, he showed her a card.

'Some fellow connected with films saw our stunt and liked it,' he told her, and there was excitement in his voice.

'But it wasn't a stunt. We were just having fun,' she protested.

'What a child you are!' he said, his voice caressing. 'I told you, Joanna, we'd go places together, and we will, you see!'

He drove away very fast, and his old car ate up the miles into what was unfamiliar but very lovely country for her.

'Where are we?' she asked, meaning which county they were in.

'Somewhere quiet, at last,' he said, pulling up and shutting off the engine.

He turned to her, and stared at her in silence for a second, and then, before her beating heart could send out a warning, he had pulled her to him and pressed his mouth down hard on hers.

She had been kissed before, but never like that. There was purpose and meaning and emotion in it, and other things, too, that she didn't understand.

When at last he let her go, he, too, looked rather upset. She had expected him to be smiling, full of confidence, faintly mocking, but he was none of these things. She was so interested in watching him, that she forgot her own distress. It struck her that he, too, was as shattered as she was over the contact of that embrace, and it puzzled her. Instinct told her that he was a very experienced young man, and the reason for his emotion was beyond her.

'You're dynamite,' he muttered, and smoothed his hair back. She watched him lean back, stretch out his long legs, and light a cigarette, drawing hard on it all the time.

She clenched her fists, to try and stop her hands from shaking, and after closing her eyes for a few seconds, her vision cleared, and that frightening excitement lessened.

'Tell me about you, Jo,' he commanded. 'I know you're an orphan, and you're supposed to come from Scotland. What else?'

'Nothing,' she shrugged.

'Where have you worked?'

'Oh, here and there, where I could. Teashops, factories, offices, any job with no training. Why?'

'Any family?'

'No.'

'Any friends, beyond our mutual pal Pixie?'

She thought of William Fenton and his mother, but instinct – that very thing which Garry himself had told her to be guided by – warned her to say nothing of them. After all, what right had she to include them among her friends? They had probably forgotten her very existence by now.

'No. Any more questions?'

'Plenty. Ever been in love before?'

'What if I have?' she flashed.

'No,' he said, with satisfaction. 'You

haven't. If you had, you wouldn't have leapt into flames as you did when I kissed you.'

He slewed round to look at her sideways, and then looked away again, as if he dare not meet her eyes for fear of stirring the fires again.

'What about you and me teaming up?' he asked softly.

Panic flashed through her. This was no proposal of marriage, she thought wildly. Suddenly she didn't want to know what he did mean. It was like putting your finger near the burning coals, but still being able to snatch it away again before you got burnt.

'What about you and me moving on?' she countered, evenly; 'I could go for a hot drink and a sandwich at a coffee stall.'

'All right.' He laughed shortly, as if he had just been putting his finger out to the fire, too, and was a little relieved that she hadn't taken from him the chance of pulling clear again.

He started the car up, and when it began eating up the miles, its humming whine seemed to soothe them both, and they eased out inside. He said, considering, 'See, we could go into pictures, it seems, with our teamwork under water. Then there's our dancing. Of course, I'm not wanting for money.'

'Just what *do* you do, Garry?' she insisted.

He laughed again. 'Well, you might say I

persuade people to talk business when they don't specially want to.'

'Oh, a commercial,' she said, in some relief, and that made him laugh again.

'What a wonderful word that is, commercial,' he ruminated, and was still chuckling, when they pulled in to a coffee stall.

'What are you doing for Christmas?' Pixie wanted to know, a week later. She accompanied her question with an elaborate air of looking everywhere and of not asking a leading question.

'If you mean has Garry suggested anything, he hasn't,' Joanna said, obligingly, as she massaged her feet.

They were in Joanna's room, their newest rendezvous. It was cosy, with the old oil stove which Pixie had pronounced as too smelly to mix with her perfumes, and Joanna had begged some threadbare grey blankets from Mrs Adey, to hang up at the window behind the thin floral curtains. Pulled across, and the light on, the room had a cosy red glow from the shade, which the enterprising Joanna had covered with red paper.

'Time he did, isn't it?' Pixie asked. 'Alec wants me to go to his mother's house, but I think that's smartening the pace up, even if Auntie would let me go. I think it'd be as well if we were to just go out for Christmas

Day, and come here Boxing Day. But he's needing a bit of persuading, on the quiet!'

'I'm leaving my job,' Joanna said suddenly. 'Can't stand being on my feet all day.'

Pixie was surprised. 'Here, don't give up a steady place till you find another berth.'

'Don't worry. I won't,' Joanna said, thinking of the offer Garry had made to her. 'Listen, if someone said to you, will you help me with my work, and wouldn't tell you what the work was, what would you do?'

'Run a mile,' Pixie said.

'No, but seriously, if someone said, it was just a bit of acting needed. Say you were asked if you'd walk into a silversmith's store, in a fur coat, sweep past the commissionaire and say you were Lady Somebody, wanting to see the best they'd got, while you waited for a friend, would you do it? If you thought you *could*, I mean?'

'Who suggested that to you?' Pixie demanded.

'Never mind,' Joanna said impatiently. 'What would you do?'

'Run like mad, if I didn't want to do a stretch. It smells to high heaven. Ask yourself, that's how the big rackets are pulled. Come on, honey, who said it to you? Who've you been mixing with, and haven't let on to me about it?'

'Saw it in a film,' Joanna said, carelessly, and was relieved when Pixie let the point go.

61

Pixie seemed to have something else on her mind, and she said presently:

'I think you and Garry had better make a foursome with us two, or heaven knows what mad idea that fool will get hold of, for the holiday. Christmas seems to be the time for people like him to go mad.'

'Did you know him last Christmas?'

'No, he didn't come here until September,' Pixie said.

'What's his work?'

'Hasn't he told you yet?'

'I got the idea he was a commercial,' Joanna said.

'He's a spiv!' Pixie said, scathingly, adding: 'But you can't help liking him, though, can you?'

They thoughtfully buffed their nails, and Joanna made cocoa with some milk in a saucepan on top of the oil stove.

'Tell you what, Jo, Alec's got a brother. Norman, he's called. Like to meet him? Nice quiet boy. Suit you fine.'

'But would I suit him?' Joanna grinned, and that set them both laughing.

'Seriously,' Pixie said, as she at last got up and prepared to go to her own room, 'I wish you'd give Garry a break for a bit. I know you're both a mad pair, and like as not get on very well together, but he's a bit – well – 'tisn't for me to say it, I suppose, but I got the feeling that he'd stop at nothing, and I

62

think you'd draw the line at safety, even if–'

'Even if what?'

'Oh, well, I know you're a good kid at heart, but sometimes it isn't easy to see straight when you've got someone as plausible as Garry Wetherall telling the tale.'

Joanna watched Pixie trail out, and sat huddled before the fire, until after midnight.

Garry didn't take her out every night. When he did, it was taken for granted that they would be home late, and Joanna got up next morning feeling tired and thick in the head. But always, up till now, she had been sure that the night out had been worth it. There were two nights in between when she could, and did, go to bed very early to make up for it.

But whether they were dancing, swimming, seeing a show or just driving through the glistening darkness in his old car, he had never kissed her like that again, nor suggested anything about their future. It was a fun-while-it-lasted sensation now, all the time.

Next day was her half-day. The café kept open all the week, so the girls had their time off staggered. Armed with a newspaper, she ticked off the advertisements which needed no experience, and did the rounds. She took the job offered last on the list, because it was late and she was tired and hungry. She came out, a little dizzy from the heat and the noise inside the factory, secure in the knowledge that for the next few weeks at least, she had a job where she would sit down all the time, and a few shillings extra in her pocket.

The factory, where she was to pack goods with three dozen other girls, was up a narrow alley off a big shopping street. In the stream of traffic outside the big shops, she caught sight of a familiar-looking car. A long-nosed gleaming monster, lined with an unusual putty coloured leather. At the wheel sat William Fenton.

She shrank back among the crowds, but in that split second, it seemed that he felt someone staring at him, and turning, saw her. He indicated a side street, and negotiated the car round there at the first movement of the traffic.

Joanna went unwillingly towards where he waited for her.

'Hop in! We can't stay here, and I want to talk to you,' he commanded.

She obediently got in beside him, and he drove round the back streets, until he found a parking space to squeeze in.

'Now then, young woman! Just the person I wanted to see!'

'Why?'

'What a question,' he laughed. 'You might have left a note or something, even if you did hate our house so much that you had to smash a window to get out of it!'

She wriggled uncomfortably.

'Oh, it wasn't that. You made me awfully comfortable, you and your mother. But I wanted to get moving. I told you so. And I'm no good at writing notes. I did try, but I tore it up.'

He smiled wryly at that. 'Not even an address where we could get in touch with you?'

'Well, why should you want to? I thought you'd have forgotten all about me,' she protested.

'You're not an easy person to forget, Joanna,' he told her. 'Now, where were you off to when I caught sight of you? Home?'

She nodded, glumly. Pixie would be out with Alec this evening, and as far as she knew, Garry wouldn't be taking her out. He had said nothing about to-night, and anyway, she was too tired. She just wanted a meal and to crawl into bed.

'From your work?' William Fenton pressed.

'No. It's my half day. I've been getting a new job.'

'Oh. Where?'

'Look,' she said. 'You're very kind and all that, but you don't want to know about me. I shall make you late if you stay here much longer. Let me get out and go–'

'I'll run you home in a minute,' he said, looking at his watch. 'It's early. I know, we'll get some tea. I know a little place–'

'No, thanks,' she said, although she was needing a cup very badly. She recalled the delicate china and the silver tea-things at his home, and guessed the sort of place he would take her to. 'I've only got my old clothes on. No, I'd rather go home.'

He smiled. 'You are a funny child. I shall go home and tell my mother I've seen you, and she'll want to know what you're doing, and everything about you, and I shall have to say that you didn't tell me anything. Sounds rather unfriendly of you, don't you think?'

'Does your mother really want to know about me?' Joanna frowned. 'Why?'

'Oddly enough, she took a fancy to you. She doesn't mind your bad humours,' he smiled.

She flushed. 'Tell her I live with friends, in the attic, in a house in a back street. They're my kind of people. I work as a waitress, and I'm switching to a packer's job in a factory. And tell her thank you for all she did, but to forget about me.'

He turned and faced her, looking critically at her.

'Joanna, that isn't good enough. You're fit for better things than that, you know.'

'No, I'm not. I know what I'm capable of.'

'Well, you can't tell me you like doing those jobs! If only you'd approached me, I

66

could have got you a nice job in the same block of offices as my own. A good old firm, needing a young woman to work her way up in the office. Wouldn't you have liked that?'

'Why should you *bother?*'

He sighed, and spread helpless hands. 'Let's get some tea. Yes, yes, don't be silly. I need some, and I'm sure you do, too.'

She let him have his way, and he drove to a quiet road behind the big shops, where there was room to park his car, and he took her through an old-fashioned alley to the side door of an old house that had been converted into a quiet teahouse. There was nothing very fashionable about it, and she breathed a sigh of relief as he found her a corner table in the pleasant main room. He didn't tell her it was one of his own properties, and she didn't ask him. She sipped her tea gratefully, and watched the stream of traffic go by outside.

'You know, Joanna, sometimes we feel pushed to do things, against our will. We don't know why we feel the urge to do them, but we do. You came into my life unceremoniously, and I'm not capable of just forgetting all about you.'

'You'd much better forget about me.'

'You're an interesting little person. I should think, with a bit of help and the right background, you'd get on very well.'

'Do you go out of your way to help every

67

young woman who comes into your life?'

'It hasn't happened before, and I don't suppose it ever will again,' he smiled. 'What are you going to do for Christmas?'

'Oh, I expect I shall go out with my friends,' she said, terrified that he'd want her to go and see his mother. She didn't know what put the thought into her head, but there was a strong feeling that his mother looked on her as a heaven-sent object to do good for, and Joanna chafed at the idea.

He called for the check at last, realizing that she was resolutely holding out against him.

'Well, Joanna, at least you must give me a note of your address. I must know where you are. No? Well, then, take this card of mine. And remember, if ever you need help, or even if you just want someone to unload your troubles on to, don't hesitate to get into touch with me.'

She dutifully took the card from him, and saw that it was one of his business cards. She shot a startled look at him as she realized that his block of offices was just round the corner from her new job. He was getting up, and didn't notice.

As they went out of the café, and went through the alley, he talked pleasantly to her about a new place he had been negotiating for, to replace the Copper Kettle, and quite suddenly he said, 'And I'm taking you home, and I don't want any argument.'

It brought her back suddenly, and she looked blank for a moment. He smiled with genuine amusement.

'You weren't listening, Joanna,' he commented, holding the door open for her.

As she went to step in beside the driver's seat, a young man stopped suddenly on the pavement, to stare at them. William Fenton looked up and followed her eyes, and raised his brows as he encountered the furious stare of Garry Wetherall.

He said nothing, however, and Joanna got in quietly enough and he shut the door. She glanced round, as William Fenton started up the car, and saw Garry still standing there, watching the car drive away. Her heart bumped unevenly, and she felt herself thinking, 'He looks ugly when he's angry!'

Joanna fled up to her room when she got in, and hoped that Garry wouldn't come home. She got out of her day clothes, into her pyjamas and the old dressing-gown, and decided to have a rest before going out to the fish and chip bar on the corner for her supper. The house was very quiet, and she had started to doze in the chair by the stove, when there was a thumping on her door.

She stumbled over to it, and opened it before she was properly awake. Garry stood there, unsmiling, his hat still on the back of his head.

'What's the matter?' she asked, blinking sleepily at him.

'Who's your friend?' he wanted to know.

'Oh. So that's it. If you want a nice cosy chat, Garry, go downstairs and wait while I get dressed,' Joanna said firmly.

'I don't want a chat. I just want to know who your friend with the car was,' Garry said, and he thrust a foot in her door.

Joanna's temper flared.

'Take that out!' she stormed. 'Take it out, and get out of here, or–'

He suddenly caught her to him again, and kissed her, a kiss of such savagery that she fell back afterwards and held a hand to her bruised mouth.

'Honey, I can find out the bloke's name myself if I want to,' he said softly. 'I just wanted to make sure you understood things. If you're going out with me, then you're going out with me, and not with a half dozen others.'

'If going out with you means I have to kick around on my own and wait your pleasure for a date, then I'm not going out with you!' she said, almost spitting out the words at him in her fury, and slamming the door before he could say another word.

She lay against it, breathing quickly, and after a second, heard him go downstairs, quietly enough. He hadn't been near her for three nights, and he still hadn't said when he was going out with her again.

Pixie came upstairs soon afterwards.

'Have you and Garry had a row, kid?'

'Why?'

'He bit my head off when I spoke to him just now, and he slammed out of the house to bring the front door off its hinges.'

Joanna hesitated. Making up her mind, she said, 'You were right. I think I will give him a rest. Is your friend Alec's brother still lonely?'

'That's the stuff,' Pixie approved. 'Leave that Garry Wetherall to cool his heels for a bit. It won't hurt him. Come on, now, put on something real smart and we'll make it a foursome. I don't need to let Alec know. We can soon rustle up Norman. Sits around all the evening with his nose in a book, and his Mum's getting worried about him.'

'Sure you don't mind? Sure you wouldn't rather be alone with Alec?' Joanna insisted.

'Oh, I like a foursome sometimes,' Pixie grinned. 'To tell you the truth, I never thought at first that you'd stick that Garry Wetherall so long, or I think I'd have thought twice about introducing you to him.'

Alec's brother Norman was indeed a quiet lad. Joanna got the impression, before the evening was half-way through, that he just didn't like girls, and would have been far happier at home with his books. However, after a quick snack, which left Joanna more hungry than before, they went to the pictures, and had something else to eat when they came out.

'Glad you came?' Pixie wanted to know, as they sat by Joanna's bedside and she told Pixie about the new job she had got.

'Oh, yes,' Joanna said truthfully, for it had taken her mind off the subject of Garry and William Fenton.

'Alec said you were a jolly good sort,' Pixie said happily, running her flaxen hair up into metal curlers. Joanna thought, with amazement, that Pixie herself experienced nothing more than a comfortable feeling, after having been out with Alec. She never looked particularly excited, or treading on air. Just comfortable. Joanna felt that she would have to get more out of courting than that.

Her doubts still lingered, until she came out of the café the next day. It was her last day there, and she was putting her pay packet away, when a young man fell into step beside her. It was Alec.

'Just happened to be passing,' he said, smiling jauntily at her.

Joanna frowned. 'How? You don't work over this way?'

'Well, as a matter of fact, I had a bit of an errand to do for the firm, and I thought to myself, Pixie's girl-friend works over here somewhere. I'll pick her up, and walk her back for company's sake, see?'

'Oh. Pixie *will* be surprised,' Joanna frowned.

'Well, I don't know as I'd mention it to her if I were you,' he said. 'You see, it's a secret, in a way. I wondered what you were doing for Christmas, and I thought I'd like to talk it over a bit, you know, fix up something nice for the four of us, and spring it on Pixie later.'

He looked a little shamefaced.

'I don't like secrets,' Joanna said bluntly, 'or surprises. Anyway, what does your brother think about it?'

'Oh, Norman!' Alec sounded faintly contemptuous. 'He doesn't think about anything but books. He wants pushing into things.'

'And are you going to push him into Christmas, as my partner, while you pair with Pixie? Was that the idea?' Joanna said, trying to get things straight.

'Not exactly,' Alec said, laughing a little. 'Well, don't look at me like that. People do swap round, and I was wondering – well, to tell you the truth, old Pixie's a good sort, but a bit stick-in-the-mud, and come to think of it, she'd just suit our Norman. They'd both jog along pretty well together. But me, now I've got ideas, and when I saw you last night, I said to myself, that's the girl for me!'

73

'Did you!' Joanna said, turning furiously on him. 'Well, I've got news for you! I don't like people fixing things for me, and I'm not the sort to let down a friend. Pixie's your girl-friend, and I'm not cutting in. Forget it, and just let me get home without company. Good *night!*'

Obviously Pixie hadn't told Alec where Joanna's new job was, for she had no difficulty the following week. The week afterwards, Christmas week, however, Pixie was rather cool in her manner.

Joanna, always blunt, said at once, 'What's wrong?'

Pixie said huffily: 'You know as well as I do!' and would say no more. On the plea of extra hard work, Pixie went to bed earlier, and they fell out of the habit of gossiping in one or other of the bedrooms before turning into bed.

Joanna fought against the obvious course. Garry had kept sedulously out of her way, sulking, she decided. Christmas loomed upon them all, with three empty days yawning, and London as lonely as it can be for people who aren't fixed up with friends and family. Joanna stopped on her way home, on Christmas Eve, and stared in a big window of the stores round the corner, from where she worked, at the creche surrounded by life-sized figures. It was beautifully done, with rich colours and subtle lighting, but it merely served to enhance her loneliness.

She suddenly made up her mind, and clutching the unwieldy parcel containing the gift she had bought for Pixie, she walked smartly back to the boarding-house, determined to make it up with Garry, and spend the Christmas holidays with him.

Pixie was coming out of the bathroom when Joanna reached the top of the stairs.

'Hallo! Have you seen Garry anywhere?' she panted, and after a second's hesitation, she thrust the package at Pixie.

Pixie, with hair in the inevitable curlers, her bathrobe trailing dismally about her, stared doubtfully at the package and said, 'What's that?'

'Oh, go in there and open it,' Joanna laughed, pushing her into her own bedroom.

Pixie struggled with the string, and gave up. 'Garry's out. What d'you want him for?'

Joanna was surprised. He should have been home some twenty minutes. 'I had a bit of a tiff with him, but I decided I'd make it up before Christmas. It's supposed to be a surprise in store for me. He's been talking about it since we first met.'

Pixie looked wary, and attacked the parcel again.

'I thought you were making a foursome with us.'

'No, not me! I never said I would!' Joanna

said decidedly, and felt Pixie thawing out visibly.

She got the wrapping off at last, and let out a yelp of delight. 'Just what I wanted!' she gasped, hugging the plaster figures of two dancers, holding high between them a Chinese lantern, in which was fixed an electric bulb. 'Now that's real smart! Your new firm make it?'

Joanna nodded, not resenting the question at all. 'Yes, I got it at cost price. They're good like that.'

'Well, I hope you'll like my present for you – you haven't got any, anyway,' Pixie said, and thrust a parcel at Joanna, containing feather-trimmed mules, in Pixie's favourite shades of lilac and purple.

While Joanna was admiring them, Pixie said diffidently: 'I was rather wondering what you'd be doing about Christmas, kid. See, that Garry Wetherall is running a red-head, but there! I suppose you know about that!'

Joanna said carefully, not looking up from the mules: 'Oh, yes,' but she hadn't known a thing about it.

'Actress, or some such thing. Getting him a part in a film swimming or something, so he was saying at supper last night,' Pixie went on, vigorously creaming her face. 'Didn't seem to care who heard about it, so I thought to myself, good for Jo! She's given him the boot so he's had to look around quick for another girl-friend. He couldn't bear to be without one for five minutes.' She looked curiously at Joanna for a second. 'Of course, you were only fooling just now, about spending Christmas with him!'

'That's about it,' Joanna said, and walking to the door, she called: 'Thanks a lot for these. Just what I wanted.'

It sounded silly, but it was all she could think of, for the moment. The thought that Garry, in a fit of pique, had taken up the chance they had both had, of film work, because of their swimming, and had flaunted his new friend around, not caring if she knew about it or not, hurt intolerably.

And all this, because he had seen her accepting a lift from William Fenton.

She sat down on the end of her bed, thinking, the mauve slippers still clutched in her hand. If she stayed at the boarding-house, that meant making a foursome with Alec and his brother, and Pixie.

She shrank away from the idea. Narrowly she had missed breaking with the good-tempered Pixie, her one friend in all the world. Obviously Pixie suspected that Alec rather liked Joanna already.

She found herself shaking her head fiercely, and putting down the slippers, she rummaged in her bag.

The old trapped feeling was upon her

again. She was being pushed into doing something she had tried to avoid. But there was nothing else for it. Finding William Fenton's card, she shrugged philosophically, and hurried out of the house in search of a telephone box.

CHAPTER THREE

William Fenton, however, was not at the office. As Joanna hung up, and came despondently out of the callbox, she happened to glance up at the clock on the church tower, and realized how late it was. Of course, the staff would have gone early, since it was Christmas Eve.

She shrugged, and began to walk quickly back to the house. She had been alone at Christmas before. It was no new experience. So long as she could put up a convincing story for Pixie, so that Pixie should not get the idea that she was evading that awful foursome with Alec and his brother Norman, that was all that really mattered. For the rest, she could find a meal out somewhere and go to a picture show, and keep herself amused until it was time to come home to bed.

She purposefully put the picture of the creche out of her mind, and decided to pretend that it wasn't Christmas at all but just another week-end to be got through, and then she saw the car. Outside the boarding-house.

She frowned, and went quietly down to

the basement. Pixie was talking animatedly to someone whose back was towards her. It was William Fenton. As he turned, Pixie saw Joanna, and shouted:

'You're a dark one, you are! Here's a friend of yours come to look you up, and you never let on!'

'Hallo, Joanna,' he said quietly, with that nice smile of his. 'I hoped I'd catch you in.'

Pixie broke in. 'And you never let me know you were all dated up for Christmas! You're a nice one, I must say! Now, I'll leave you two alone because I'm sure you've got lots to talk about but I'll be back to make a nice cupper, so don't be too long gossiping!' and with an arch look she went out of the kitchen to find her aunt.

Joanna, scarlet as a beetroot, said: 'How did you find out where I lived?'

'I asked your firm for the address, since you omitted to supply it yourself.'

'But I never told you the name of–'

He laughed softly. 'You said they were near where I found you that day, and that they made plaster lamps. It wasn't difficult to locate the only firm of that description in that small area.'

'Well, now you've found me, what did you want me for?'

'Don't be truculent with me, Joanna. I told you before, I wasn't satisfied about the way you were going to spend Christmas. I'm still not satisfied.'

'I'll be all right. I'm spending it with Pixie and her friends.'

'But your friend Pixie tells me that you've turned down her invitation in favour of me.'

Joanna, still scarlet, said, 'Oh, let's get out of here. I can't talk here. There's something I wanted to ask you.'

'All right, we'll go out to the car.'

It was easier to talk to him out of hearing range of Pixie and the others. She had heard whispering in the scullery and knew that Pixie's aunt was interested now. She couldn't blame them for being interested. So little happened in their lives.

'I'm in rather a spot,' she said, staring ahead at the long string of lights which lit up the curving length of Cedars Street. 'I *was* going out with Pixie and her friend and his brother only – well, it's so stupid. Her friend met me from work and said he wanted to change round. Go out with me, and fix Pixie up with his brother. He's being tiresome, and – well, I didn't tell Pixie. She'd be so hurt.'

'And so you've backed out of the arrangement altogether.'

'I didn't know what else to do.'

'What about the young man we saw that day?'

She turned sharply to look at him. She had hoped that William Fenton hadn't noticed Garry's ugly stare that day as she had got in his car.

'Oh, he's just a friend.'

'And what did you want to ask me, Joanna?' he said smoothly, thinking that Garry Wetherall probably considered himself as much more than a friend, to judge by the proprietary way he had looked at her.

'I wondered if you were running any all-over-Christmas services at one of your café places,' she said slowly. 'And if so, you'd probably need a pair of extra hands. I'd like that. Something to keep me busy over the holidays. Christmas is a silly holiday, really, especially when it comes at the week-end. It's too long.'

'I see. Yes, I've three or four. I've just bought a small hotel, too, where we might fit you in. Tell me, have you ever had a really jolly Christmas in your short life, Joanna?'

'Oh, well, noisy parties at neighbours' houses, but they seem a bit silly, too. Presents and eating and being noisy, and drinking, too. It doesn't seem to have much to do with—' and she broke off, wishing she hadn't said so much.

'With what?'

'Oh, nothing,' she said, with scorched cheeks. Not to anyone could she bring herself to speak of the creche. That was private and personal.

'You weren't thinking of the first Christmas, by any chance, Joanna?' he murmured, as if divining her thoughts.

'What about the job over Christmas?' she asked roughly.

'Never mind that, for the moment. I wonder whether you'd do something for me?'

'Yes, of course! If I can,' she said doubtfully.

'Well, it's a funny thing I'm going to ask you. I know you've been wondering why I've been moving heaven and earth to keep in touch with you, and I suspect that that independent soul of yours is chafing at it like mad. The fact is, you're the elusive shadow of something I've been pursuing for years.'

He smiled at her puzzled face.

'You don't understand that, do you? What I'm getting at is, I'm fed-up with the sort of Christmases we have at home. The conventional Christmas. Would it be too tiresome if I asked you to help me find the real thing somewhere? I don't know where I'm going to look for it. But it won't be at Pevensey House, any more than in this street. How about it, Joanna?'

'What about your mother?' the practical side of her insisted, though her eyes danced in anticipation.

'My mother has a large house-party, relations and very dull people. I think she won't miss me very much. I'll phone her.'

'What about that Elaine?'

He laughed softly. 'That Elaine will be there,' he assured her. 'You don't like her.'

'I don't think you do much,' Joanna said frankly, and that made him laugh again.

'Go and say good-bye to your friends,' he told her. 'And don't be long.'

Pixie wanted to know where they were going. That was inevitable.

'I don't know. It's a mad surprise sort of Christmas,' Joanna said, but there was a high flame in her cheeks and her eyes were blazing with excitement.

'Well, you can't go like that!' Pixie protested. 'Come on upstairs and get into some decent things, while I pack a bag for you. Of course you want a bag – don't you want to scrub your teeth, and sleep?'

Misgivings began to flood in, and Joanna wondered if she had done the right thing in saying yes to William Fenton. Much better if she'd pressed for that waitress job.

Pixie put into the bag all Joanna's best things, the few new things she had been gathering from her wages since she had been in London. Joanna, playing for safety, put on her black skirt and jersey, because no matter how mad William Fenton might become in the next day or so, he was after all, still William Fenton, and hardly likely to appreciate the purple outfit which Pixie was again pressing her to borrow.

'He looks real nice,' Pixie observed. 'Rich, too. Did you know he's the boss of Pevensey Properties?'

'What on earth's that?' Joanna asked blankly.

'If you don't know what Pevensey Properties means, you don't use your eyes,' Pixie said warmly. 'Why, you can't take two steps anywhere without falling over something or other owned by them! He must be so rich, why, he must *bath* in the stuff!'

She thrust into Joanna's hold-all her own best jar of bath salts, and tin of matching talc. 'There you are, honey. That's to you from me, with all my good wishes. It's not your Christmas present, just a make-weight. Here's your real present – nylons, cut-price from Alec's place. You can do with 'em.'

She watched Joanna curiously as the girl took them and stammered out her thanks. Pixie, good-hearted though she was, was not usually as generous as this.

'Fancy you picking a rich pal like that,' Pixie went on, pursuing a train of thought. 'The bloke who rescued you from the snowstorm, I suppose.'

Joanna nodded.

'Well, have a good time, but remember everything I told you,' Pixie cautioned her, and pushed her to the stairs. 'Don't keep him waiting, girl, he's too precious!'

Joanna hesitated as she reached the car, and William held the door open for her. He looked at the hold-all and nodded.

'You'll need that,' he said.

'It wasn't my idea,' she protested. 'I thought you'd be bringing me back to-night. I don't know what you told Pixie—'

'Hop in,' he said briefly.

'I thought we'd go and get a meal first,' he said. 'And by the way, Joanna, as this is going to be a rather unusual holiday, you'd better stop calling me Mr Fenton. It rather reduces everything to normal, and we don't want that, do we?'

'What shall I call you, then?'

'Could you manage "William", do you think?'

She wasn't looking at him, so she didn't see the tiny amused smile quirking his lips, especially when she shook her head at that, with determination.

Pixie's conversation, with its stressing how very rich he was, had rather dashed her, and she felt that a lot of the gilt off this sudden and promising spree had been tarnished. She had known that he was quite well-off, but not as rich as Pixie had seemed to think.

'No, it *is* a bit much,' he admitted ruefully.

'Have you got any other handles?' Joanna wanted to know.

'Well, what do *you* think? When I was a helpless baby they decided to call me

William Pevensey Jacques de Mandeville. Nothing much I can do about it, is there?'

'Well, stone the crows!' Joanna observed, with feeling. 'Wouldn't "Bill" do?'

A huge smile spread over his face as he turned to look at her. 'No one's ever called me Bill, Joanna!'

London was glittering, artificial. Crowds thronged the pavements, there were too many Christmas trees used for decorating the big stores, too many hard bright lights, too much noise. After fruitlessly searching for a quiet place to eat, he said: 'Joanna, are you hungry, or can you wait half an hour? I've thought of a place!'

'Where?'

'About half an hour's run out. It's an inn. The Three Jolly Sailors. We'll get a good meal there.'

'You don't own it, do you?' she asked him.

'I don't own any inns,' he assured her.

The quiet cloak of the countryside hung over the place, and the lights were soft and warm and yellow. In an old-fashioned parlour they had an excellent meal and some wine, and then he leaned forward and said: 'I've got another idea. Do you know a place called White Cross Corner?'

'I don't know this side of the border,' she reminded him, her brown eyes sleepily happy in the warmth of the room.

'Up you get, Joanna. You need fresh air. You've eaten too much,' he said, and when they were in the car, he told her: 'White Cross Corner's completely rural, completely unspoiled. I think we'll find Christmas there.'

She slid down in the seat with a sigh. Contentment slid over her. He glanced sideways and half nodded with satisfaction.

'I thought you were a product of the town,' he observed.

'Oh, I love town, most times. But not for Christmas. I don't know,' she said, moving restlessly. 'I don't know myself very much yet, I suppose. Does one, ever? Do you know you, Bill?'

'No. I've never had time to find out. You're going to help me find out what sort of person I am.'

'When? Now?'

'Now's as good a time as any. All my life I've moved to a pattern. Doing as the others did. School, college, then the firm. Board meetings, dictating letters, leaving the office to attend concerts or sedate dinners. How do you have *fun*, Joanna?'

She whooped with laughter, and slewed round to look at him. 'You wouldn't want my sort of fun, Bill!'

'What sort?'

'Oh, fair-grounds and noise, and wearing old clothes, and doing just as you like, and not having to know anyone or remember your manners. Oh, pictures and music-halls and rides on tops of buses, and swimming and cycling and picnics and coffee-stalls–'

She broke off to look at him speculatively. What would he want to know all about that for? 'You wouldn't like it,' she said, her laughter gone.

'Try me, and see. On Boxing Day we'll search for a circus. Ever seen a really big show?'

'No,' she breathed. 'Not the big slap-up kind!' On consideration, she said: 'You won't do it. You have to book seats weeks ahead. You can't just break in like that.'

'I think I could manage it,' he told her, with a smile.

White Cross Corner lay off the main road. He swung the big car into a narrow lane and took a humpback bridge with speed, making Joanna jerk up in her seat with a surprised squeak. 'Like the scenic railway,' she exclaimed delightedly.

At the end of the village, beyond the thin straggle of thatched roofs, a little square-towered church stood, commanding a view of the main street. It was getting late, and the lighted windows of the cottages sent out bars of red light across the little street. He pulled the car up in front of one of them, and in the silence after the high whine of the motor, he said quietly: 'What about Mid-

89

night Mass?'

'Oh, yes. Yes,' she breathed.

'We've just got time for a visit first,' he told her, getting out.

She followed him up a little front path through a typical cottage garden, and waited while he thundered on a little green door. Then they were in a warmly lit room, and a wiry little woman with iron-grey hair twirled into a minute bun on top of her head, lifted floury hands out of a pastry bowl, and nervously wiped them on a cloth, as she looked first at the person who had opened the door, and then at William Fenton.

'Why, bless us, it's Master Will!' she exclaimed at last.

'You didn't know me, Nannie,' he accused, enfolding her in a great hug. 'This is my dear old nurse,' he told Joanna as he introduced her.

There was a bright coal fire with a black kettle singing at the end of a chain, and Nannie was making mince pies. Her daughter Charlotte, who had also been in Mrs Fenton's service before she married, was making hot ginger wine, the children tucked into bed. Holly and evergreens protruded from the tops of the many picture frames round the wall, and people came and went. Joanna sat by the fire, listening to family gossip and village talk, until William said it was time to be getting over to the church.

'Where will you be sleeping, Master Will?'

'We simply hadn't given it a thought, Nannie,' he said, with a kind of crazy happiness.

The old woman clucked her tongue at him, very much as she must have done when he was little. 'Tom, run over to the Bear and see what they can do about a room. We can shift up a bit and make room for the young lady here, if she doesn't mind a squash, but we can't fit you in nohow, Master Will.'

'There isn't much of the night left, or there won't be,' he told them. 'Anywhere will do.'

People were trickling out of the houses to the church, and Joanna said happily: 'Oh, it's starting to snow. A white Christmas, Bill!'

The little church had white stone walls and a few fine stained glass windows. It was so small that the service had an intimate quality, and the white-haired vicar seemed to be talking to each one of them personally. Joanna, whose memories of church had been a kind of duty visit each Sunday to Sunday school, in order to secure the required number of marks for a free ticket to the annual treat, found in this service something new.

'It's the trappings,' she told herself fiercely.

'The lighted creche outside and the Christmas Trees inside. It wouldn't seem like this at any other time,' and she glanced at William Fenton, and surprised a rapt look in his eyes that she hadn't imagined could be there. She looked away quickly, as if she had been eavesdropping, spying. She had no business to see that look, she felt.

All of a sudden she felt miserable. This was all make-believe, she told herself, biting her lip, unable to join in the carol singing for the lump in her throat. She thought of Rorton, and her grandfather, the young man she had gone out with, and who had turned out to be a thief; Garry, and the job she still didn't know much about, but which seemed to bring him in a lot of money; Pixie and her friends, and the people she worked with at the factory.

William Fenton's hand closed over hers, in a big, powerful grip, and looking up she found an inscrutable expression on his face. She forced a smile, which broadened in answer to his own.

It was snowing thickly when they came out. William said: 'Come on, what's going on in that funny little head of yours?'

She thrust her chin upwards, and felt the snow, cool and soft, on her skin. 'It isn't anything to do with us, is it, all that in there? It's – well, a bit like heaven, I suppose. You get a glimpse of it, and then you come out again, and it's the same old round again. A big smudgy, even if it isn't really black, but all that in there is so clean,' she said, jerking a head back towards the church.

He nodded slowly. 'I know what you mean, Joanna,' he said softly, and held her hand tightly as they walked back to his old nurse's cottage.

There was a great quantity of Christmassy food, and hot drinks, and subdued laughter – mainly because of the children asleep just above their heads – and then the waits came and softly sang outside. And they came in and had hot drinks, and no one seemed to realize that it was so late.

When William took his leave, they were saying 'Happy Christmas' all round, but it was a different kind of noisiness from anything which Joanna had previously experienced. Here was sincerity. No one was being noisy for the sake of being noisy. She struggled to find words to express it, but couldn't. She went to the door with William, and he showed her where the Bear was; a fine specimen of architecture, a typical ancient inn, across the road. The snow lay thick on the swinging sign outside, and although the bars were closed, lights streamed out from the upper windows.

'I shall be over early in the morning to pick you up, Joanna,' he smiled.

'What are we going to do?'

'What a child you are!' he murmured. 'I expect we'll see the children open their parcels, and by that time I'll have thought up something else. Joanna,' he said, in a changed voice, 'I haven't got a Christmas gift for you.'

'Oh, yes, you have,' she said, with shining eyes. 'You've given it to me already.'

'Oh. What was that?'

She pulled a funny little face. 'A magic ticket into a new world. I'll have to go back, of course. Everyone does. It can't last. But I'll have the memory for always.'

He bent towards her, but she fled back into the front garden of the cottage, calling 'Happy Christmas' over her shoulder.

He watched her thoughtfully, as she stamped her feet to clear the snow, before bursting into the front room and the warmth and light, before the green door shut on her and blotted her out from his sight.

It was a white world they woke to, the next day. Joanna stretched her arms above her head, in the tiny room with the half sloping ceiling, and watched the thick flakes softly falling past her window. This was very much the same weather as when she had gone to Pevensey House.

She frowned. She didn't want to think of that place. It struck her as odd and out of keeping with William's character that he could break away like this, from his home and friends, and his mother. She wondered what Mrs Fenton would say when she knew (if he ever told her) how he had spent Christmas. Joanna didn't believe that Mrs Fenton had really taken a fancy to her individually. She was however, prepared to believe that Mrs Fenton would be enchanted with any young person who happened on her doorstep and gave her the opportunity to be kind and helpful.

She thrust the thought of Pevensey House and William's mother from her mind, and thought about this day and the whole of to-morrow, which presumably she and William would spend more or less alone together. She didn't attempt to analyse her feelings towards him, but allowed herself to be carried along on this tide of new excitement.

Before they left the cottage, Joanna had a confused impression of small children, and parcels, wrappings, string and Christmas cards, a Christmas tree filled with home-made parcels and decorations, and a good breakfast which had none of that greasy smell overpowering everything near it, which was the order of the day at Pixie's aunt's boarding-house.

William said, starting up the car: 'I believe you didn't want to leave them!'

'They're nice people,' Joanna sighed.

'What was your old nurse talking to you about, in the scullery?'

'She was reminding me about old Mrs Copthorne. She used to be the gardener's wife. Now she's a widow and living in Northchurch Wyck. It seems there's a fine example of sixteenth century barn there, going for a song.'

'Oh, are we going to look over property?' Joanna said, disappointed.

He laughed softly. 'You don't know how interesting it can be, young woman. Wait till you see it.'

'We're looking for Christmas, aren't we? Looking over barns belongs to every day,' she said stormily.

'Little firebrand. All right, we won't do that. You're right, of course. I can't expect you to be interested in those things.'

Old Mrs Copthorne was tiny and dark and wizened, and had shrewd black eyes like boot buttons. She looked Joanna over, and although she spoke civilly enough, Joanna felt that she was privately deciding that here was not a fit person to be going about with the beloved Mr Will. Nevertheless, she made them welcome in the centre of her family, but Joanna didn't like these people so much as the old nurse's family.

Uneasiness rose in her as one of the sons said abruptly: 'I've seen you before!' and he didn't sound civil at all.

His mother said, 'That will do, Ben. The young lady's with our Master Will,' and that silenced his tongue, but not his eyes. They kept sweeping her in an accusing glance, and Joanna was afraid he would recall the newspaper photograph before long.

She was patently eager to be going, so William rose before he intended to, and hadn't time to mention the barn that was to be auctioned. He was a little disappointed. He had hoped to be able to take Joanna over it, and show her what was for him an all-absorbing topic.

From there they attended a tiny church where angelic looking children were singing in a choir, and later in the day they came across an out-of-the-way village where there was an ox being roasted in the open, and Christmas puddings being presented to the old people. But the magic of their Christmas had faded a little, by a pair of stranger's eyes resting on Joanna with suspicion and recollection.

'Joanna, what did that chap mean?' William asked testily.

She wriggled in her seat and said: 'Heaven knows. Should I know why he said that?'

William stopped the car. 'Ever since I've known you, there's been a secret look in those eyes of yours, and I've always felt it oughtn't to be there, somehow. I don't know what happened to you before I met you, but

I feel somehow that if you could tell me now, I could put a stop to it, whatever it was, so that you didn't have to run away from people.'

'Who says I'm running away?' she demanded, her voice rising.

He didn't reply, but merely raised his eyebrows significantly. That he could convey his meaning with such brevity of action and scarcity of words was a thing she didn't understand and which infuriated her.

'I didn't like those people!' she said sullenly, after a silence in which she felt that the last vestiges of the magic were swiftly slipping away.

He answered fairly enough. 'That was my fault. I couldn't expect you to, but I forgot that. You see, the Copthornes are all tied up with my childhood and happy memories. My method of chasing Christmas was to delve into old memories of some very happy times, but of course, I forgot that people change. Nannie hasn't but the Copthornes apparently have. We'll do something else, shall we?'

'If you like,' she said.

'There's nothing you want to tell me first, Joanna?'

'I came with you to get away from my life, not to stir it up,' was the rather unsatisfactory answer she offered him.

The magic had abated for him, too, and he

couldn't see how or why. Because of that deflated feeling, he did something he hadn't been meaning to.

'I telephoned my mother this morning, Joanna. Just to wish her the season's greetings.'

She swung round suspiciously.

'What did you do that for? Did she want to know where you were?'

'She did. I did it out of filial affection. She was delighted to hear who my companion was.'

'She wants you to go home,' Joanna said flatly.

'Joanna,' he laughed. 'I'm not a boy. No, my mother said she would be delighted to welcome you if I cared to bring you back for what was left of the holiday. I think it might be a good idea.'

'No!' she stormed. 'If you've had enough and want to go home, jolly well go, but don't think you're going to drag me back there with you to be patronized by everyone!'

He looked hurt, but had no comment to make on that.

He said instead: 'What went wrong, my dear? Where did we manage to spoil it all, and how?'

She shook her head, and despite her best efforts, the tears would well up in her eyes. It had always been like this for her. Whenever a nice patch came along, something cropped up from the past to spoil it.

He leaned towards her and took her hands. She didn't look at him, but stared through a mist of tears at the whiteness of the surrounding country, and the untrammelled snowy surface of the road ahead of them, where they had not defiled it by tyre marks.

'Joanna,' he said slowly, 'however much we may rebel against it, I feel that Fate has, for reasons of her own, flung us two together. I think we shall see a lot of each other in the future. I don't know why, or indeed how. But that being so, don't you think we ought to be perfectly frank with each other, from the start?'

'I don't believe in Fate and all that rubbish,' she muttered, blinking fiercely and biting hard on her lip. 'Life is what you make it. If I've made a muddle of mine, that's my business, and I don't have to tell anyone about it, if I don't want to.'

He sighed and let go of her hands. 'That's all right, if no one knows. But I have a feeling that there are some people who know, and those people may not necessarily be your friends. For your own safety, you should let a friend have the same advantage.'

She was silent for a minute, and then shook her head angrily.

'All right,' he said, starting up the car again. 'If that's the way you feel, Joanna, there's nothing I can do about it. I suppose that's why you don't want to go to Pevensey House.'

'What d'you mean?' she flared.

He shrugged. 'I don't know what it's all about, but it seems to me that you're afraid of someone there. After all, you left us in the middle of the night. Hardly the action of someone with a clear conscience.'

'I'm not afraid!' she stormed.

She watched the mileage dial and thought about the people at William's home. Dr Lindsay wouldn't be there, so why shouldn't she go, just for this once, just to show him she had nothing to be afraid of?

'All right, I'll come,' she said, in that surly tone which at once infuriated and amused him. 'I suppose you'll say I'm being rude to your mother if I don't.'

He patted her knee. 'That's the girl,' he approved, quietly.

But when they arrived at Pevensey House, Joanna was at once sorry she had come. Although William's mother was delightful and gracious to her, the other guests were not so sweet. There was Elaine Sellers, looking particularly well-groomed, and the pretty Lavinia Durrance, who came forward and was affectionate in a restrained way to William. All as if they accepted him by right and Joanna was an interloper. And leaning casually against the radiogram was Dr Lindsay, in casual tweeds, looking as if he had every right to be there.

'We've only a small party now, dear, so we can be nice and cosy,' Mrs Fenton said, making a place by the log fire for Joanna to sit near her. 'Now what have you two sly people been doing for Christmas?'

'Where on earth did you sleep?' Elaine drawled.

Joanna said, 'Together, under a hedge, of course!' which made Elaine scowl and Lavinia look shocked. But Joanna was sorry she had said it, the minute it was out, because of the way Mrs Fenton looked, and the pained expression on William's face.

'Well, where did she think we slept?' Joanna said furiously.

The doctor had a suspicious quirk round his mouth as if he wanted to laugh outright, but he didn't. They called him Charles, as if he were one of the family, and Joanna had a faint recollection of this happening when she was ill in bed, although at the time she noticed very little at first.

He, oddly enough, went out of his way to be nice to Joanna, though when she was alone at one end of the room he did come up to her and say in a low tone, 'Well, how's life treating *you?*' which Joanna construed to mean, 'What a nerve to come back here, with me knowing what I do!'

The whole long day was filled with tiny incidents which chafed, mainly from the two girls and their antagonism. Little things which perhaps William's mother didn't notice, but Joanna was quick to bite on. She was half deciding she would go back to London, when she heard Charles Lindsay say from across the wide hall to the butler, 'Let it go, Branson! Shut up, man, this is Christmas!'

Branson looked bothered, coughed slightly, and said: 'I'd like to, sir, but it's more than I dare do, them feeling as they do below-stairs. I must let Mr William know!'

Joanna tried to see out from behind the velvet curtains, where she had been curled up in a great window seat, staring out at the snowy landscape and wondering why she had been fool enough to come here. They couldn't see her, and she knew she ought to come out before it was too late, but it wasn't in her to do that. All her life's training had been to stay quiet and find out what she could, rather than come out into the open and lose everything. Like a little animal, she played canny.

'Show me what you've got,' Dr Lindsay said roughly. Then, almost at once, he said, 'Oh, that thing again! How on earth did you come by that?'

'Well, sir, one of the under housemaids was wrapping something up in it. It was just an old newspaper. But the picture, d'you see, sir, it's the young lady right enough, isn't it? Same name and all? There was uproar at once, sir!'

Joanna's heart turned over. That wretched newspaper again – why did it have to be that particular one?

'Give it to me. I'll tell them about it later. Not now,' Charles Lindsay said, and would no doubt have taken the newspaper and kept it out of sight, but William Fenton happened to come out of the library at that moment.

'Have you seen Joanna, Charles?'

The butler and Charles Lindsay looked at him, and he knew something was wrong.

'What's the trouble?' he asked.

Joanna waited, and heard the rustle of the offending newspaper. She waited with baited breath, and heard William say, haughtily:

'Well, what of it? It's all finished now, quite satisfactorily.'

'Good lord, did you know about it, old man?' Charles Lindsay asked.

'Naturally. We all did,' William Fenton said coldly.

Joanna slid back behind the heavy curtains, and closed her eyes. She decided that he had done an elaborate bit of face-saving, and she took her hat off to him. It had also saved her from a painful scene. But what was to happen now? Obviously she couldn't stay here any longer.

She heard them go away, in different

directions. The big hall was painfully silent, as if people, ghosts of the past, were breathing quietly, near her. She shivered, and found herself hating this house, because of a fancied animosity in the very bricks and stones of it. She didn't belong here. Why on earth didn't she get out and stay out?

A voice, very near her, said suddenly, in an angry low tone, 'Well, haven't you even the decency to show yourself, or are you going to hide behind that curtain indefinitely?' and William Fenton thrust it back with one jerk of his arm. In his other hand was the newspaper, and from it, her own photograph grinned back mockingly at her.

CHAPTER FOUR

They faced each other in cold fury, and then Joanna spat out: 'I didn't want to come here, but you made me! I knew what it would be like, but it turned out even worse. It isn't enough for those precious friends of yours to insult me. Even your servants have joined in.'

'Can you wonder?' he asked, equally angry, but quieter. 'This isn't a desirable thing to–'

'Desirable!' she took him up derisively. 'That's all you think about, you and your kind. What is *desirable*, and what isn't! Well, I'm not a desirable person. I told you so from the first. I never wanted to come to this house when you found me in the snow. I got out of it as soon as I could. Then what did you do? Kept on till you found me and then wouldn't leave me alone. You and your looking for Christmas!'

She got off the window seat and stood facing him, tilting her chin up so that she could meet his look squarely.

'And don't think I'm going to give you all the inside dope buckshee, because I'm not. If you want to know what really did happen, you can jolly well work hard to find out. You don't seem to have much else to do!'

'I ask you to tell me, from the first, if you were in trouble. Apparently I'm good enough to fill up a date that's fallen through, but not good enough to have your confidences. What did Dr Lindsay do to qualify?'

'Oh, yes. I'd forgotten him,' Joanna said, her eyes widening. 'Your precious pal, who muscles in among his patients for Christmas. He threatened me, so I had to tell him about it, or he'd have called in the police. I suppose he thought it wasn't worth the candle, when the whole thing fell through.'

'I'm rather dense. I still don't know what it's all about.'

'No, you wouldn't. You don't speak to anyone until they're vetted and their past lives are pronounced O.K. I'm not like that. If I'm lonely and someone offers me friendship, I take it. How was I to know the police were after him? For all I know, he's quite a decent chap, just had bad luck, the same as I did.'

'No, Joanna!' The wintry smile fled, and William Fenton almost shouted at her, he was so shocked. 'You mustn't say things like that. You mustn't even think them. It's so wrong. You'll go on being in trouble if you think that way. Luck has nothing to do with it!'

'Oh, hasn't it! That's all *you* know!'

'It's what you are, that counts. No matter how badly things go with you, you simply must do what is right, keep on the right side of the law. If you're starving, it doesn't mean that you have to become a criminal.'

'You haven't been starving ever, so you don't know what you're talking about.'

'Oh, we can't stay out here. Come along in with the others,' he said, reading deadlock in her mutinous little face.

'Who, me? In there with that lot? Are you off your head? Why, you'd have a strike in your kitchen if I were to go in there!'

'Don't be silly, Joanna. I've assured Branson that it's all right.'

'Why did you?' She grinned. 'Ashamed of the company you keep?'

'Protective towards you, I suppose, but you wouldn't understand that, would you, Joanna?'

'I don't understand anything except that I hate this place, and I'm going, and don't you try to stop me.'

He watched her go upstairs, to collect her things from the room allotted to her, and shrugged slightly. When she came down, carrying her one small case, he was waiting for her, with his topcoat on ready. As he opened the door, she saw the car swing round to the front.

'You'll say good-bye, won't you, while I'm

108

keeping the engine running, Joanna?'

'They know I'm going?' she asked blankly.

'I told my mother that we had only really looked in to say hallo, and not with any intention of staying. She was disappointed, of course.'

'I'm not saying any good-byes because I'm not coming here again, and you needn't bother with speeding the parting guest. I'll get a lift on the highway.'

But it wasn't so easy to get her own way with William Fenton. He didn't insist on an unwilling good-bye, but he did take her things and pilot her into the car before she could protest. His quiet manner rather floored her, because beneath it, beneath the polished good manners, was an iron will. It inspired her to fight against it, because she always fought against opposition, but she found she was left without weapons. It was no good kicking and screaming with someone who achieved his object without raising his voice. She understood Garry Wetherall far better than William Fenton.

As they drove back on the main road to London, he said to her: 'Is it really all over, Joanna? This business with the police?'

'There never was any business with the police. They just wanted to ask me things about *him*, because I'd been with him just before he disappeared. They didn't want me when they found him.'

'But how did they get hold of your photograph to put in the newspapers?'

'We both stayed at the same boarding-house. People talk. I suppose they searched my room after I'd gone. That was one of a sheet of tiny pictures – oh, you wouldn't know the sort I mean.'

'I might,' he said frostily. 'What made you run away, if you'd nothing to fear?'

She shrugged. 'It was something he said.' She hesitated. Confidences never came easily to her. 'He was swanking a bit about a way of making easy money. He said something about a job the night before. And he acted scared when a policeman came near him. Not much to you, I suppose, but I recognized the signs. I was born in a port. You wouldn't know.'

He sighed. 'And so you ran away. Didn't you know that if you'd stayed to face the police and told them all you knew, they'd have been satisfied?'

Her face showed the gamut of emotions. Blank surprise, derision, frank – and rather pitying – amusement. 'Oh, well, if that's what you think–' she said, shrugging, and nothing he could say would move her in that deep-rooted belief.

Finally he pulled up at the side of a grass verge, and got out a cigarette. He looked frustrated.

Looking curiously at him, she asked: 'I

don't get it! Why should you *care?*'

'I don't suppose if I explained for a million years, you'd understand, little Joanna.'

'You mean you still like me?'

He laughed shortly. 'Whether I like you or not has little to do with it, I'm afraid.'

'Then you're sorry for me!' she accused. 'You're full of good works, like your mother!'

He coloured angrily, but said nothing, and continued to stare ahead.

'Oh, take your back hair down and slosh me one, for that!' she begged. 'I should know where I was then.'

'You know where you are now, Joanna, but you won't admit it. On the one hand, you have us, my mother and myself, offering you a solid friendship, which as far as I can see, has nothing wrong with it beyond the tiresome verbal intrusions of friends, and that happens everywhere. On the other hand you have the people you live and work with and–'

'What's wrong with them?' Joanna demanded fiercely.

'Oh, I expect they're good-natured and helping and all that, but none the less (and you won't in all honesty be able to deny this you know!) they have a very casual way of looking at the difference between right and wrong.'

'If you mean they're thieves and swindlers, then–'

'There you go, you see! They probably don't ever commit a crime as such, but wouldn't object to being smart occasionally, or telling something that wasn't a lie but not the absolute truth.'

'What's wrong with that?' she wanted to know.

'Everything. And such people are especially bad for you, because it seems to me that with your background, you haven't had a chance, and you never will have. Joanna, Joanna, if you'd had a decent background, you'd think twice before you ever accepted friendship from an unknown man, however lonely you were!'

'You're a fine one to talk about pick-ups!' she retorted coolly and grinned with appreciation at the flush of anger that again darkened his skin.

'You're distorting the truth, as I explained just now,' he said, after a moment of damping down his annoyance. 'I wasn't wanting an evening's pleasure with you. I merely wanted to help you by means of a lift, on a very unpleasant day. That's different.'

They wrangled all the way to Town. William Fenton patiently explaining, begging her to consider giving up her unfortunate friends and let him get her into a reputable firm and find decent lodgings, spending the week-ends under the care of his mother; Joanna, fiercely defending her

own kind, insisting on her absolute independence, both in finding a job and somewhere to live, and in finding companions
and background for leisure. And in this
mood of deadlock they parted at the end of
Cedars Street.

'Sure you won't let me run you to the gate,
Joanna?'

'No thanks.'

'Joanna, this is still Boxing Day,' he
reminded her. 'Let's have another shot at–'

'–finding Christmas?' she mocked. 'No,
thanks. It turned out a flop, as I ought to
have seen it would. Don't worry, I'll find
something to do for the next few hours.'

She fled down the slushy street to the area
steps, and vanished from his sight.

She let herself in with her key, but the house
was in darkness, and absolute silence. She
wandered through the empty floors, pausing
at each landing to listen, and realized that
everyone must have made some sort of
plans for spending to-day out, once the
mid-day meal was over. There had been
some talk of Mrs Adey going to the Rose
and Crown to see her friend, and spend the
rest of the day there 'where there was a bit
of life', and this was to happen once
everything was washed up and cleared away.
Pixie, she recalled, would be somewhere
with Alec. Heaven knew where Garry was.

Her room looked rather forlorn and was certainly bitterly cold. She abandoned the idea of lighting the oil stove and staying there, and having dumped her bag, she ran downstairs to go out and mingle with the crowds in the West End. There would be little back street cafés open and she could join a queue for a show somewhere, she decided.

As she was opening the front door, she heard a key scrape cautiously in the lock. Garry, very surprised, stood on the top step outside.

'What d'you think you're doing?' she demanded. 'Boarders aren't supposed to have keys.'

'I found it,' he said quickly, sticking his tongue in his cheek. 'Back from your rich friends already?'

'The holiday's almost over any way, and I only came back for something,' she said, stung.

He raked her with his eyes, pushed her backwards, came in and shut the door. 'I didn't see the car anywhere, so it seems your rich pal hasn't waited for you,' he murmured, and pulled her roughly to him.

She pushed him off. 'What's the idea? The last time we met, I thought we decided we'd call the whole thing off?'

'Oh, think nothing of it, honey. I was a bear with a sore head that day. I'm sorry.

114

See, I'm apologizing handsomely. Now, tell you what, I'll take you on a spree, just to make up and show how sorry I am.'

'With your redhead?'

He chuckled. 'Jealous? Good sign, baby, a very good sign.'

'No, I'm not jealous. I just don't like a crowd. Anyway, the same applies to you as to me. Like you said to me, if you're going out with me, then you're going out with me and not with a dozen other girls.'

'Fair enough,' he said, pushing his hat to the back of his head. 'What about What's-his-name, who's been trailing you around over Christmas?'

'I don't know, and I don't care. We just didn't see eye to eye, so I walked out on him. That goes for anyone who upsets me.'

He grinned appreciatively. 'That's what I like about you, kid, your spirit. Don't you let anyone knock it out of you. Besides, a fight now and then livens things up a bit.'

'What were you going to do, if I hadn't been here, Garry?' she demanded, thinking of the key in his hand.

He played with it, and put it back into his pocket. 'It happens to be mine. I got it made from one of those on the board downstairs. Want to make something of it?'

Joanna thought of the things William Fenton had been saying to her on that miserable journey back from Pevensey

House, and in an odd sort of way it gave her a savage pleasure to find that they were true, and that she had a mind to stay on what he called the wrong side of the fence.

'No. I don't think so. Having made a spare key for yourself, why go to so much trouble? Pixie would have let you in.'

'She couldn't. Not to-day, seeing as she isn't here. Nor is anyone else, come to that.'

'Oh, wanted the place to yourself, Garry, to pinch things.'

'Don't be so upstage, girl. Not a bit of it. I just wanted a bit of a look round, while the old girl was away. Just a look-see, to find out what she guards with her life. For your information, she's only tootled for half an hour. See what I mean?'

'All right. You wanted a look. Don't let me stop you,' Joanna said.

'While you – do what?' he asked, narrowing his eyes.

'Go out for some fun. I haven't had any yet. Been preached at by a lot of stuffed shirts in a house that looks like a museum. If you want a look round anywhere, why not pick a place like that, where there'd be something to see?'

'Maybe I will, at that,' he said, taking her arm.

'Where d'you think you're off to, Garry?'

'To take you around, give you some excitement, and keep you out of harm's way, Jo.'

'Supposing I don't want your company?'

'What would you do on your own?'

'Take the first likely offer of male company that happened along.'

He chuckled. 'That's just what I thought. You're mad enough to do anything to-night.'

He had parked his car temporarily in a mews entrance. He bundled her in. 'We'll have a real spot of fun. I know just what you want.'

'Anything but the circus,' she said, quickly, recalling the suggestion which William Fenton had made.

'Circus?' He was shocked. 'I'm not giving you kid's stuff to-night, girl,' he told her, and began to laugh.

There was a mad light in his eyes. He pulled up in a back street and took Joanna up five flights of stairs, and knocked a curious kind of knock on a shabby, un-numbered door. A girl looking as blousy as Pixie did first thing in the morning, opened it. At the sight of her, Joanna felt curiously comfortable. She was so much like Pixie.

'Fix us up, Lou,' Garry said. 'We going on a trail.'

She grinned, and opened the door wider. Before they left the place, the girl had found a short dance dress in an old gold taffeta, and a short fur jacket, for Joanna. While she was fixing ear-studs into position, Garry came from another door, in evening dress.

He looked devilish and exciting, and stood looking critically at Joanna.

'She'll do,' he pronounced. 'Go easy on that perfume.'

Lou looked approvingly at her work, and went back to a table littered with drinks and over-spilling ash trays. 'Have a good time, bless you,' she said, and lost interest in them.

Garry said, 'Come on. Now for some fun,' and took Joanna back to the car.

'She's not all that kind. What made her do this?' Joanna asked frowning.

'Sort of paying off of a debt she owes me, shall we say?' Garry laughed mockingly.

'Oh, say mind-your-own-business and have done with it,' Joanna said, irritably, and relapsed into sullen silence until they pulled out in front of a tall old house with a red carpet rolled out to the kerb.

'But this is Mayfair,' she protested.

'Right first time, Jo, and this is a swell party.'

Joanna's heart thudded a little. 'We're gate-crashing,' she told herself feverishly, and thought of William Fenton.

'We can't go in, Garry. We haven't been invited.'

'Oh, yes, we have, but we left the invitations behind,' he said, and started to laugh.

The cars moved on, and they were borne in on a tide of people in similar dress.

Joanna heard Garry say something as they went in, and a name yelled out above the din. No one took any notice. No one stopped them as they tried to dance in the compressed dancing space, and drinks and cocktail snacks were pressed on them as well as everyone else. Joanna, high on the tide of the curious excitement she had experienced before with Garry, found herself thinking feverishly. 'We're not stealing anything. Just a little fun, and no one'll miss that.'

Then Garry said, 'Let's go. The fun's over.'

They got their coats and went. There was still a lot of coming and going. He got his car from somewhere in a remarkably quick space of time. They were whirled away from the bright lights, before she realized what had happened.

'Am I supposed to ask why we came away?' she asked tartly.

'Oh, it was beginning to pall. Besides, there was a blooming engagement going to be announced any moment.' He grinned lop-sidedly at her, and said no more.

'Where are we going now?' she demanded, as the lights twinkled on dark water beneath them.

'I bet you think a river's just there for tugs and barges to be on,' he teased.

'And for slipping away at night, and for police launches,' she retorted, and that seemed to dash him for a moment.

'Now, don't spoil it, honey,' he said, pulling up the car at the edge of a wharf and looking over the edge. 'Ah, yes, here it is. Put on that old raincoat in the back of the car, and look sharp about it.'

She did as he instructed, and followed him down a narrow flight of slippery stone steps, to where a small motor launch lay at the bottom. He got in, and stood balanced, handing her down.

'Now, for some fun,' he said madly, opening up the throttle. 'Hold your breath, baby!'

Flying spray, intense cold, and a heady sensation that was more potent than champagne, filled Joanna. As she hung on tightly and got brief glimpses of keyside landmarks flashing by, she had a sense of well-being that blotted out all other considerations. Something was vaguely wrong about it. It wasn't Garry's boat. She was wearing clothes that weren't hers. It was a stolen evening. But none of those considerations mattered. She was *living*, and Garry was the one person who could elevate her to these heights.

He stopped the little craft some way up the river.

'Are we out of petrol or something?' she gasped, wiping her face.

'No,' he said easily, leaning against the little cabin structure to light a cigarette, and then stared at the stars.

Joanna followed his gaze. The night sky was hard and bright. All the stars in the heavens, it seemed, were there, looking down on them brilliantly and impersonally. The impersonal gaze of that night sky frightened her, and she looked down quickly at the fast-flowing river. The stars were so aloof and serene, and somehow so *right*. So tied up with a feeling which had eluded her, and which had sprung out of that service in the little church, at midnight, when William had been by her side.

She thrust her little face up to Garry. 'You're *fun* to be with!' she muttered.

He threw his cigarette away, and caught her to him. The movement rocked the little craft, but he steadied it, and pressed his lips down to hers. The kiss was long and hard, but it was without satisfaction. It was what she had wanted, and he had understood, but it had left her as restless and as longing as ever.

He stared at her, puzzled.

'Not getting any ideas about your new pal, are you? Young Rockefeller?' he asked roughly.

'What if I am?' she retorted. 'We made a bargain, didn't we – or as good as? No other hangers-on while we go out together.'

He nodded, and appeared contented. Obviously his mind was on something else, and when he said suddenly: 'Kid, would you do something for me, something special, if I were to ask it?'

'Of course!' she said, recklessly. Nothing mattered, at that moment, but to cock a snook at that remote sky, and all it stood for. 'Just say what you want!'

His eyes gleamed, but he shook his head slowly. 'When the moment comes, I'll let you know. Right now, we'll go on with the medicine. It's doing you good, I can see that. Fun's what you need!'

But it wasn't. She knew that, as she felt the rush of stinging air on her face, and the cold needle-points of spray from the river. She needed something, but it wasn't fun. It wasn't anything which Garry could give her.

The uneasiness which she had been pressing down all the evening heightened as he shut off the motor and floated cautiously in to the side. Looking over the edge, just his eyes level with the stone causeway of the wharf, he saw all he needed to, it appeared, and hastily ducked. He pushed the boat quietly down river until they reached the next stairs, and after tying up rather casually, he got her up and they both stood hiding behind a pile of timber until the two dark figures moved off down river to where they had last heard the chug-chugging of the little motor. As soon as they had gone, Garry whispered: 'Run for it.'

As he swung the car out through the timbered buildings, Joanna remembered another night rather like this, and anger seared in her. There was no need for this. They had been on a spree at someone else's expense, and it would have served them right if the police had caught them. But that other night was lost in the mists of childhood. It hadn't been a spree. She couldn't remember whom she had been with, but there were others, and some of them had got caught.

She suddenly felt wretched and ashamed. Without knowing it, she made the decision then, which coloured her actions the next morning. She had not meant to go into anything without Garry. They had made a pact to stand by each other. The fact that he had let her down before, mattered little. They were together now. Nevertheless, when she was offered the glittering post of mannequin at a well-known Mayfair house, even if it was only to fill a place for the time being, she took it, on the spur of the moment, without once referring to Garry. The fact that it had arisen from someone seeing her in the glamorous swimsuit he had provided, mattered little. It was doubtful if she thought about Garry at all, at that moment. Her one thought was, as always, in a crisis: an escape, a getaway. Not only from Garry and his way of life, and the strange hold he had on her, but from Pixie and the boarding-house, and moreover, from William. Most of all, from William. Away from William and his straight thinking, and from her friends and their far from straight thinking, she felt that by taking the middle course, and staying on her own, she would get a little peace of mind.

CHAPTER FIVE

Pixie had had a disappointing Christmas. She told Joanna about it, at some length, that next evening.

'D'you think Alec is cooling off me?' she thrust at Joanna.

With an effort, Joanna brought her thoughts back to the little attic bedroom with its smoking oil stove, and Pixie sitting curled up on the foot of the truckle bed. Pixie looked anxious, and absently stroked at her face, smeared with wrinkle cream, as she waited for Joanna's reply.

'Do you like Norman?' Joanna asked suddenly, without quite knowing why.

'Lor, what a question!' Pixie observed with feeling. 'He's dead from the neck up.'

'But you wanted me to have him,' Joanna pointed out.

Pixie had the grace to redden.

'Not permanent, ducks. No, I'd never wish that on my best enemy. But just to help you over laying off that Garry Wetherall. That's all Norman's for, really. To help a girl over her troubles with her own man.'

'That's what I mean,' Joanna nodded. 'Cultivate Norman and make Alec sit up a bit.'

Pixie chuckled with appreciation of the tables being turned on her. 'Now that's what I call real smart! I might expect it of you, kid. D'you know. I began to wonder if you were getting all upstage, just for a bit, you know. This last week or two, you haven't been like our Jo at all.'

'How?' Joanna asked, guardedly.

'Kind of quiet, as if you were thinking a lot.'

'Even I have to think sometimes, Pix,' Joanna said, absently.

'Well, stop buffing your nails and tell us what you're thinking about now, and while you're on the job, how about letting us know what you did over Christmas – or is it a secret?'

'I told you – I went down to Pevensey House and got bored stiff, then I came up and spent Boxing Night with Garry.'

'Lor, I never believed you when you told me you'd been out with that skunk again!' Pixie observed, with intense feeling.

'He's all right,' Joanna said, off-handedly. 'To tell you the truth, I just had a few hours on my hands. Pixie, would your aunt be offended if I said I was packing up?'

'Here, what's all this?' Pixie demanded, abandoning the wrinkle cream, and forgetting to pursue the subject of Garry Wetherall.

'I got a job to-day. A new one. A good one.

But the only thing is, it's live-in. The digs go with the job and the good pay and I can't afford to sniff at any of it.'

Pixie considered the point, and unwillingly conceded that it was sound sense. 'But where is this fancy job? How did you get it? When does it start? What have you been so cagey about it for?'

Joanna grinned. 'How about one question at a time!' she murmured, swinging her legs down, and getting up to make the inevitable cocoa.

'Don't think you can get out of answering like that, kid,' Pixie warned.

'I'm not,' Joanna said impatiently. 'I'll tell you everything about it, except where it is.'

She stirred in the boiling milk, and shrugged her shoulders. 'It's no use looking like that, Pixie. You and your aunt are the best pals I've got, and I'm not saying I wouldn't trust you with my life. But you know this place as well as I do. Just you tell your aunt where I've gone, and like as not that Garry (or someone else?) will just happen to be listening, and I might as well go and tell him in the first place. Don't you *see?*'

Pixie sat back in vast comprehension. 'Oh, it's *him* you don't want to know about it! I'm jolly glad you've come to your senses about him at last! Still you could write your address down, I suppose, so's I could write to you!'

'And have him come across it?' Joanna returned scathingly. 'Make no mistakes about it, there's nothing in this house he doesn't know about, and I think you know it!' She played with the idea of telling Pixie about the extra door key he had had made, and at the last moment clung loyally to him and didn't say a word about it. After all, there was nothing in this house worth taking, and anyway, Pixie would soon be out of it. Joanna could see that. Pixie was on the warpath to get married, now that the unfortunate Alec was beginning to show signs of cooling off. For Pixie, the fun was over, and she'd have to haul in the line before she lost the fish.

It depressed Joanna a little. She thought of Pixie in some small boarding-house, getting fat and unshapely like her aunt, and having no fun. Padding to and from the sink to the gas-stove, even smelling of the constant frying in oil, and getting tired and old.

'What would you do, if you were married to Alec?' she asked suddenly, coming to the end of her details about her new job.

Pixie looked gloomy. 'Stay here and help Auntie, or open up a boarding-house not too far away.'

'Does Alec want that?'

'No, that's just it.' She hesitated, and then wiping off the cream with tissues, said despondently, 'He's got big ideas. It's speed-way racing, at the moment. Motor cycle mad, he is. Get-rich-quick mad, too. Wish he wasn't like it. Wish he was more like Norman, straight I do!'

'Does he know Garry Wetherall?'

She didn't know why she had asked that question. It was just one of those things that popped into her head without reason. More of an intuition, a warning with that cold little flutter of fear in its train.

'Of course he does. Seen him here, hasn't he?' Pixie snorted, but she, too, looked alarmed.

'Keep 'em apart, if I were you,' Joanna muttered.

'I don't need telling,' Pixie said vehemently. 'Easier said than done. That Garry Wetherall, he ought to be shipped overseas somewhere, out of harm's way. All it wants, now, is for him to get Alec one of those smart jobs he's always talking about.' A thought struck her. 'Kid, you haven't said how you got into this posh West End salon yourself. Them jobs don't grow on trees. You didn't let Garry get it for you, I suppose? No, of course you didn't, or else you wouldn't want him not to know your address. Well, who *did* get it for you?'

Joanna wriggled her toes in the warmth, and hesitated before replying. There were things she had told Pixie, as a friend and confidante, but there were also some she had omitted to tell Pixie, and it always needed a little thought before speaking, to make sure she didn't trip herself up. Pixie forgot nothing, despite her vague expression.

'Seems someone saw me once when I was out with Garry. I must confess I don't remember his face. Smart-looking customer. Gave me his card and said I was to turn up at one for the interview. Well, it meant going without lunch, and nothing might come of it, but there were a couple of dozen others after the job so it made me feel better. I got it.'

'Why?' Pixie, the materialist, demanded.

Joanna said: 'Would you say I was unusual-looking?'

'Watch your step, kid. There's always a catch in it when they tell you things like that!'

'What, in front of two dozen other girls?' Joanna repudiated, scornfully. 'Don't be daft! No, he'd got a funny-looking collection of clothes there, to be tried on, and I must say they didn't look as if they belonged to any of the others. Tall and stately and not half bad-looking, they were. I was on the small side, and they did seem as if they were cut out for me.'

'Oh. Well, you know best, kid. Got a bit beyond my advice lately, I'm thinking.'

'Well, what *would* you advise me to do?

Chuck it, just because it wasn't an advert in the paper? What's the difference? You can get funny business in an advert for a waitress or machine minder, you know!'

At that point, it struck Joanna that Pixie was merely being arbitrary. She didn't want Joanna to go away, nor did she want her to take a chance on getting a highly paid job in the West End. Mutinously, she stuck her chin up and said, with finality, 'And so I'm taking a chance!'

She wouldn't give Pixie an address, but told her she would write from time to time, and that when she had the chance, she would say where she would meet Pixie, for lunch, or perhaps tea and a film show. Pixie, bristling with suspicion, had to agree.

Florian's was approached by the staff through a mews entrance. An incredibly dreary back door led to draughty back passages which reminded Joanna of a small Northern theatre. But the showrooms were the last word in magnificence.

Florian was a little man, tiny and dark, with a wizened old face and eyes that saw only the lines of a gown's flowing. He nodded several times and clicked his tongue, and put Joanna in clothes which he called 'piquant', 'saucy', 'gamin' and 'daring'. Joanna thought it all a lot of nonsense, got inordinately tired the first few days, did a great deal of running about for the other

131

mannequins, and took part in small shows, to see how she shaped up. Florian himself presented no terrors to her, but the manager, who had engaged her in the first instance, worried her.

The other girls noticed it, too. Joanna shared a room with two other girls, and called herself Joanna Lee. No one questioned it. No one wanted to know where she had come from, but they did want to know where she was going. It was always the future, the glistening, beckoning future, which filled the conversation and thought of these girls. They all set out to captivate the rich clients who came to the shows, and their main source of bitterness was that most of the clients were women, without escort.

'Did you know Len Savage before you came here?' one girl, a languorous blonde with tilting almond eyes, asked suddenly one evening, as they were all grooming themselves to turn in early before the big show next day.

'No,' Joanna said, easily, without thinking. She didn't like the manager much, not only because of the uneasiness he filled her with, but because he was the ruthless type which always prompted her to want to give battle. In this place, she divined early on that a mannequin did not fight, but calmly accepted things. There were too many of them, one wouldn't be missed. And Len Savage had no hesitation in saying goodbye to any of them.

'Well, he takes a special interest in you,' Gloria continued. 'And it almost seems parental.'

There was a ripple of soft laughter, but it wasn't unfriendly laughter.

Joanna flushed, but didn't retort. With an effort, she gave the friendly kind of answer which Gloria had to accept. Gloria would be a bad enemy, she knew instinctively.

'Isn't he parental, as a rule?'

'Darling!' There was again that soft ripple of laughter. 'Don't be juvenile. He's a wolf and you know it, or you wouldn't have that special look he dotes on and calls such fancy names. But oddly enough, he isn't a wolf with you. I think you must be his kid sister or something.'

'Maybe I'm just not his type, but he doesn't think I'm harmful,' Joanna murmured, trying to fasten down that elusive thought that had come into her mind when Len Savage first saw her and gave her his card.

That had been just after Christmas. January came and went, and the first show in February brought an influx of male clients with the women.

She watched, from the fitting-room, down through the curtains on the balcony, to the curving wrought iron staircase, where Gloria was trailing in a filmy negligée, and a willowy brunette was following in a nightgown that was a dream. She herself had on a naughty little street outfit that was somehow too clever for general use, and relied solely on its cut for its success.

As she followed Gloria with her eyes, she saw a group of people among the seated clients who seemed familiar to her. Only when she had taken the staircase, were her suspicions confirmed. Elaine Sellers, with Lavinia, and William's mother. She couldn't see William anywhere, and she was thankful for that.

As she paraded past them, Elaine recognized her. She saw the leap of recognition in the girl's eyes, and she recalled with dismay that she hadn't given her proper name here, and that one of the Pevensey House party would surely ask Len Savage about her.

As she paraded back, Mrs Fenton called her over. 'Why, Joanna, dear, I couldn't believe my eyes! How lovely you look!'

Len Savage, hovering, as always, came over, and talked about the outfit. He made Joanna peel off the jacket, the dress top, the little pleated skirt, and made her hitch, with embarrassed fumbling fingers, the accordion-pleated evening skirt with the fur trimmings, which went with, and transformed the set.

While she pirouetted and performed, feeling more like a helpless animal in the circus than the girl whom William had taken out over Christmas, she heard Elaine, Lavinia and Mrs Fenton murmuring how clever it all was. And then a dissentient voice cut across it all, and Joanna saw, for the first time, that there was a fourth member of the party. A graceful little old lady with beautifully dressed white hair, and a pair of wicked blue eyes that missed nothing.

'I think it's an absurd outfit!' she declared. 'What a parcel of nonsense the whole idea is. Street outfit into evening dress, indeed! It only needed to be made up in tweed–'

'It *is* tweed, Lady Lonsdyke,' Florian purred, coming up at that moment. 'Tweed interwoven with plastic – the newest thing, and the fur is plastic, also.'

Lady Lonsdyke registered good-humoured disgust, which discomfited the rest of her party. Catching the old lady's eye, Joanna lost her sense of confusion, and wanted madly to laugh. She bit her lip, and looked up at the ceiling, and was thankful when Florian waved her away. She found herself wishing, as she mounted the staircase in the wake of Gloria still in the negligée, that William had been there also. Would he have found it as embarrassing as his mother had, or would he have laughed with Lady Lonsdyke?

Len Savage kept her after the other girls had gone.

He was holding a large white envelope, with an impressive-looking seal on the back, and he absently played with it, tapping it on the edge of his chair, and looking speculatively at her.

'Joanna Lee, is it?' he murmured.

Joanna's heart sank. Had they told him she was Joanna Roberts, after all?

She nodded miserably.

'I didn't know you had influential friends,' he murmured, still pleasant enough in his manner.

'I'm a girl who makes friends where I can, sir,' she murmured.

'Quite right,' he approved. 'Do you look on me as a friend?'

Feeling on dangerous ground, she shook her head. 'As a very fair employer,' she said, instead.

That delighted him. 'Very clever! Very good indeed! Now, I think we must try and arrange something else for you. You made a hit with the clients to-day. Several asked who you were, and wanted you to show off other things. We can't have favourites, you know, but, well, we must please our clients.'

She nodded again.

'Mustn't we?' he persisted.

'Whatever you and Monsieur Florian say,

'must be right,' she said, wishing he would come to the point and let her go.

'Oh, Florian doesn't bother with the domestic side of the business. He leaves that to me. But I see the clients' point, Joanna. You really are a delightful little creature. Tell me are you seeing your friends to-night? Oh, well, perhaps you'd better read this letter first – it may be an invitation.'

He gave her the letter and waited.

'Where were you before you came here, Joanna?' he murmured as she struggled to open the thick embossed envelope.

'In a factory,' she muttered, without giving the matter much thought. It was the one thing she had meant to hide. He repeated it, smiling still, and passed to her Florian's jewelled letter-opener.

'I'm sorry,' she gasped, covered with embarrassment.

'What for?'

'For having letters – I know it isn't allowed–'

'Oh, rubbish! Lady Lonsdyke is very rich and important. One of the few clients who does and says as she pleases,' he said, smiling broadly.

She opened the letter, and read in bewilderment: 'Joanna, dear, you will not remember me. I saw you when you were asleep. It amused me inordinately that you played such a good joke on my dear but over-serious friends at Pevensey House. Come and see me at my hotel – I shall be there three more days. I have an idea that you and I may have something of interest for each other.'

Joanna shook her head slightly. Had she imagined it, or did Mrs Fenton say that she had brought one or two friends up to see her when she was ill (and apparently her niece) but that Joanna had not awakened in time?

Len Savage asked smoothly, 'An invitation for to-night?' and putting out a lazy hand, took the letter from her.

'Here, that's mine!' Joanna said, her voice rising above its carefully modulated usual pitch, and she snatched at the letter. Still smiling, he held it out of her reach.

'Temper, temper,' he reproved. 'You shall have it when I've read it. Um,' he muttered, handing it back to her. 'And what does all that mean?'

'I haven't the foggiest. She must have mistaken me for someone else.'

'I think she did,' he agreed pleasantly. 'I'm certain her ladyship made a mistake. You see, she referred to you as Joanna Roberts.'

Joanna turned the envelope over, but it was addressed merely to 'Miss Joanna', after the prevailing fashion at Florian's. Joanna didn't know the surnames of the other girls.

'We'd better go and see her to-night, and find out,' he said. 'Yes, you must have an escort. It will be my duty and pleasure to take you. Let me see, the white evening dress, I think.'

He stood off and considered her, and finally shook his head. 'No. White suggests, even in these modern times, innocence. No, we must find something else.'

'I wish you'd forget the whole thing, sir. I don't want to go and see her. I'm sure she's made a mistake. I'm Joanna Lee.'

'I know what we'll do,' he said, 'we'll try an experiment. Charlotte's leaving us. If you look well in the Chinese model, you shall have her place. Yes, yes! Even Florian will approve of that!'

The Chinese model was in stiff brocade, with a pattern of dragons and lotus buds all over it. The tunic was long and straight and smoky mauvish greys and dark jades mingled with gold thread work, into a very rich design. It was slit at the bottom at intervals to allow the movement of a fine pleated full underskirt in the pinky-mauve tone of the lotus buds, and there were little Chinese slippers to go with it. It had a subtle admixture of East and West, which, coupled with Joanna's dark eyes and hair, and her petite figure, was at once provocative and innocent, wicked and simple.

'I hate it!' she said, in a low tone, as Len Savage propelled her to the mirrors.

'Perfect,' he murmured, ignoring her.

'Florian will want to design something for you only. And to think he raved about Charlotte!'

'I won't go!' she stormed, suddenly forgetting and raising her voice.

Len Savage said, keeping his voice deliberately low-toned: 'But you will, my dear. I've just remembered where I'd seen you, before you blossomed out in the dragon swimsuit. Yes, you'll come with me, I think.'

Florian's blessing had to go with his latest creation.

'No, no, no!' he cried, wringing his hands. 'Not with that hair. Lacquer! Oh, no, no, it would never stay down! Well, then, we must defile my creation by the cap. Yes, yes, that will do, I believe. We must hide that awful hair.'

Joanna, protesting still, went with Len Savage in Florian's second-best limousine, to the hotel where Lady Lonsdyke was staying. On her head was the small jewelled brocade skull cap which reminded her of the bell of a flower, or at worst, a Chinese lantern.

On her arms, bare to the cape-like stiffened sleeves of the tunic, were beaten silver and copper bangles of Eastern design to match the ear-rings they had clipped on, and there was a haunting suggestion of oriental perfume.

'We'll dine quietly,' Len Savage said,

looking rather splendid in tails.

They were taken upstairs to a beautiful room, where a table was set for two.

'Is this Lady Lonsdyke's suite?' Joanna gasped.

'I thought you weren't anxious to see her?' Len Savage smiled.

'Aren't you afraid I shall spill soup or wine on Florian's horror?' she asked, maliciously, crumpling her full red lips into a wicked little smile.

Len Savage looked startled for a moment, and then interest flared up in that perfect face of his, and the gleam which Garry had sometimes had, came into his eyes. That gleam, reminding her so strongly of Garry when he meant funny business, brought back all the old uneasiness.

Len Savage said, under his breath, 'Heaven help you if you do,' but she hardly heard him. *This,* she told herself, *is a private room he's hired. Lady Lonsdyke's out, or not here at all.* Panic rose higher as she cursed herself for being such a fool. But where, along the line, she had gone wrong, she couldn't say. The bringing in of Florian to bless the evening had been a masterstroke, and one which had completely disarmed her. She thought dully that Len Savage would probably get her so tight that she'd be only too glad to take off the precious Chinese creation. It was heavy, and hot. She wondered dazedly who would ever buy the thing, or if indeed it had never been designed for sale but rather for advertisement.

Dignity, she told herself, passionately. *Have a bit of dignity.* Who had said that? William. What would William think of her for being in this predicament? She felt her cheeks growing hot at the thought, and tried to concentrate on the movements of the waiter, and the wine waiter. Champagne bubbled, and she wondered if Florian knew about all this, and whether it had been put down to the expense of the firm.

'Drink up, Joanna. A toast to the future, and may it be a brilliant one,' Len said smiling.

She sipped her champagne and put the glass down. She was too worried to be hungry, and yet somehow she got through the excellent meal. After all, she told herself, it would be so easy to get up and walk out, while the waiters were still coming in and out. Short of clubbing her, what could Len Savage do? Her background ensured that she took one view and one view only, of that. She would be running away in a priceless creation. How easy to call for police help, and a cry of 'Stop, thief!' She couldn't imagine in whose name he had hired the room, or whether he was known. She only knew the old trapped feeling. And then her panic subsided. How easy it would be. All she had to do was to practise the old trick of looking for the Ladies' Room and forgetting to come back.

Len Savage talked easily all the time, discussed wines with the waiter, referred to Joanna's taste and smoothly answered for her and he watched her.

When the meal was at last wheeled out, he got up and locked the door quietly behind the waiters. And he turned and said, still smiling: 'In case that wary look in your eyes means that you'll soon be going to the Ladies' Room, Joanna, forget it. It's over there. This is a suite, self-contained.'

Joanna sat back in her chair. In one stunned moment, she saw herself running from the man in Sunderland, to pitch into friendship with Garry, cutting loose from Garry to take a nose-dive into this. She told herself, savagely, that she needed a collar and chain, to keep her out of trouble.

'Aren't you forgetting my friend, Lady Lonsdyke?' she asked sharply.

He shook his head. 'You don't use your eyes, my poppet. She's a long way away.'

'But this is her hotel—'

'On the contrary, it's my hotel. Hers is quite some way away, and all you needed to do was to take the trouble to look up at the name in neon lights, but you didn't. You were so trusting.'

Her face flamed. 'You wait till I tell Florian

to-morrow,' she spat out.

He bowed slightly. 'I *am* Florian. Oh, you mean my dress designer. Oh, he hasn't much weight. A clever fellow, but interested only in needle and thread. Think nothing more about it.'

'You're Florian?' she gasped.

'I've always found it a pleasant fiction to pretend to be only the manager. Poor Florian has to answer for a lot of things, according to me, while I am a kindly fellow who would do more for people if only I were the boss, but alas, I am but the manager.'

'I don't believe it!' she flared, trying to rack her brains and remember what the girls had said about Len Savage and what, if anything, they had said about little Florian, or whatever his name really was. It struck her that they had not even mentioned the designer, and few of them bothered to even look at him. Did they all know, then? Had they all, at some time or other, awakened interest in Len Savage, and had this sort of experience? Or hadn't he bothered about them? Had Charlotte been here before, and was that why she was leaving, now Len Savage's interest was elsewhere?

'Let's not waste any more time,' he said. 'I've a lot to – er – say to you. But first, cut along to the bathroom, like a good girl, and get out of that outfit. I don't much mind what foolishness you get up to, so far as your person is concerned, but that creation is, after all, exclusive and worth quite a lot of money.'

'Besides, I can't go far in my petticoat, I suppose!' Joanna retorted, with something of her old spirit.

He smiled appreciatively at that, and stood dangling the key-chain from his pocket, swinging it slightly, speculatively. She shut herself in the bathroom, a breathlessly beautiful room in lilac and gold, but found to her chagrin that there was no way of bolting or locking the door.

She scowled at herself in the mirror, and ripped off the jewelled cap, ruffling her hair until it stood out like a golliwog's wig all over her head. In a boiling rage at her own stupidity, she tore off the tunic, and then stared thoughtfully at the pinky-mauve underskirt, with its simple low-cut top of mauve silk and the narrow shoulder straps. Fingering the lilac bath-towel behind the door, her eyes gleamed.

'Having trouble with the fastenings?' Len Savage's voice sounded anxiously at the door, and the handle rattled.

'No, I'm not. Your precious outfit's intact, but I'm so damned hot and sticky, you'll have to wait,' she flared, turning on all the taps at once. She dragged a heavy bath-seat in front of the door, under cover of the noise of the water, and flung up the window, to find to her intense relief, a little runway behind a low wall of cement, where apparently the electric light sign was erected.

With the lilac towel flung casually round her shoulders like a stole, she edged her way along the parapet, thankful for the little cement wall, and for the flat Chinese slippers. Once round the corner of the building, she found a fire escape, and a taxi, and this time asked clearly and distinctly for Lady Lonsdyke's hotel.

In the back of the taxi she found she was shivering uncontrollably. She closed her eyes, and told herself fiercely that there was nothing the matter with her. It was just the aftermath of edging along that parapet. But it wasn't just that. It was the situation she had got herself into this time. Once before, she had been alone and adrift in the snow, without luggage, but she had had outdoor clothing on, her handbag, and some small change in it. Now she had nothing, nothing in the wide world but an evening underslip, a bath-towel and a pair of Chinese slippers.

CHAPTER SIX

Joanna thought that to the end of her life, she would never forget the expression on Lady Lonsdyke's face when she first saw her.

She said thickly: 'I can't pay the cab, I haven't any money,' and stopped, because her teeth were chattering.

She heard Lady Lonsdyke tell someone to 'see to it', and then, as on that other occasion, everything blacked out, and the floor rushed up to meet her.

When she came to, she asked: 'Am I going to have pneumonia again?'

She was lying on a couch before an electric fire. Lady Lonsdyke, with a glass in her hand, said dryly: 'I doubt it. The trouble with you young people is that you take excitement like strong drink, and don't know when you've had enough. Here, get this down, and you'll feel better. Now perhaps you'd better tell me all about it.'

Joanna began, haltingly. Words weren't her strong point. Finally she was put off because Lady Lonsdyke began to laugh.

'Not at you, my dear, but at poor Florian.'

'Did you know *he* was really Florian?'

Joanna gasped.

'Heavens, yes. It's an open secret among the clients. I imagine he uses it as much to subdue the staff as for anything. Now, what are you going to do with yourself? You have no job, and nowhere to go, as far as I can see.'

'Oh, I suppose I can go back to Cedars Street,' Joanna frowned. That needed explanations, too, and she began to get bored.

'Oh, yes, I know how you feel!' Lady Lonsdyke murmured, nodding her head. 'It's a wretched nuisance trying to paint a picture for the other person to see. But I must know what ties you have, before I make you a proposition.'

Joanna remembered the note, and flushed a little. It was hardly the best time to burst in on someone, without making an appointment first. She noticed, for the first time, that Lady Lonsdyke had her dressing-gown on, and her beautiful hair was pinned into place ready for the night.

'You'd better stay here with me for to-night,' Lady Lonsdyke nodded. 'I'll arrange a room for you. You can't go back to this Cedars Street place for to-night. Besides, what about the young man. Garry Wetherall. Where does he fit in?'

'He'll be furious.'

'Oh. Why?'

'We did rather agree to share things. Anything that came out of the swimming pool evening. He provided the swimsuit, you see. Oh, it isn't as awful as it sounds. He just made me a present of it. No strings,' Joanna finished miserably, thinking how odd it was that it had never sounded quite so awful before. It depended, she supposed, on who you were recounting the story to.

Lady Lonsdyke said: 'He sounds rather an adventurer to me. I think a clean break would be healthy, whether you want it or not. You seem too nice a child to be allowed to penetrate further into this curious half-and-half existence that the young man seems to specialize in.'

'It isn't like that–' Joanna began.

'You haven't a thing to wear, so I hardly think you'll escape from here before I see you again. Even you'd be hardly likely to wander about in broad daylight in that unsuitable get-up! Now, off to bed you go, and you can take breakfast with me. Then we'll discuss things in more detail.'

Lady Lonsdyke wrote to her great friend, Mary Fenton: 'She's pretty and gamin, unconsciously impudent, and altogether splendid material to keep me occupied for the next twelve months. Owing, I believe, to the outrageous trick she played on our friend Florian, she seems ready enough to fall in with the idea of accompanying me on

149

my world tour. Whether, however, she realizes that I am embarking on making the proverbial silk purse out of very rough material, is quite another matter, and one on which I do not propose to dwell for the moment. Sufficient, I think, to be able to get her out of England before the inevitable rebellion comes.'

Mary Fenton, at breakfast with Elaine and William, took off her horn-rimmed glasses and said: 'One never knows what to expect of dear Agnes, from one day's duration to another.'

Elaine smothered a yawn and said nothing, and expressed little interest when Mary Fenton passed the letter to William. William choked over reading it, looked very angry, and passed it back without a word. And so Elaine knew nothing about what had happened to Joanna until months had passed, and Joanna was photographed with Lady Lonsdyke at a party in New York.

That photograph caused a lot of trouble. Up till then, the watchful Lady Lonsdyke had managed to steer Joanna clear of press photographers, if she hadn't managed to keep her out of mischief. At Mary Fenton's request, but as much to please herself as to comply with that, Lady Lonsdyke had reported each month on the interesting experiment which she had started.

Beginning with France, in conventional

fashion, she had bought Joanna simple clothes in Paris, taken her on a motor tour to the Riviera, and endeavoured to show her the quiet side of France which she herself loved, rather than the fashionable side.

'Joanna looked as if she was going to defeat me at the outset,' Lady Lonsdyke wrote, from the safety of the Alps en route to Switzerland. 'She endured dressmaker's fittings and dutifully wore her simple new clothes. Then she ran away. I was in an agony of anxiety, until I found her modelling in Pierre's new salon in Rue Parnel. How she managed it without a word of French, I don't know! As always, with Joanna, I hardly know whether to die with rage or laughter.'

In Switzerland, Lady Lonsdyke wrote anxiously: 'Joanna is not twenty yet. I have got the reluctant truth from her. She is a bare nineteen, and she led me to think she was nearly of age. However, my lawyer tells me there is simply no one in that ghastly Scottish town where she lived, who cares what happens to her, so I have washed my hands of that aspect. There is another which is equally alarming. She collects young men as a jar of jam collects wasps, but she doesn't seem to care for them. It is excitement itself, not young men, which goes to her head.'

William was more worried than his mother and Lady Lonsdyke when he read that. 'I wish I could get away,' he fumed. 'I'd give a lot to dash over to Switzerland and talk to her.'

'Who, dear? Agnes Lonsdyke?'

'No, Mother! Joanna, of course!'

'You like her, don't you, William, dear?' she said, gently, and sighed. It had been a sharp disappointment to her that he hadn't made a match of it with that nice Lavinia Durrance, whose parents were such old friends of hers. 'We know nothing about little Joanna at all.'

'Oh, yes, we do,' he said savagely. 'If you'd only some *idea* of her background, if you'd only *seen* those awful people in Cedars Street–'

'Where *is* Cedars Street?' she asked faintly.

'It's a London back street. One of those big, faded, one-time Georgian rows of properties, shockingly neglected. Hopeless place. Tenements, mainly. The aunt had a sort of boarding-house, so-called–'

'What sort,' she persevered, 'and whose aunt? Joanna's?'

'No, the aunt of this friend of Joanna's, who'd been living next door to her in Rorton. And don't ask me where Rorton is, Mother. It's a port, just over the Scottish border. Mother, if you'd only some *idea* of Joanna's background, you'd share with me the conviction that she's come out of it all pretty well, and that with just a bit of help, she'd–'

'I hope you aren't going to say what I think you are, William,' his mother said faintly. 'Anyway, a world tour with Agnes Lonsdyke is the most marvellous piece of luck for her, or for any girl, come to that.'

'Joanna isn't *any* girl!' he retorted.

'Oh, isn't she, William?'

'And I really don't think that Lady Lonsdyke is a fit and proper person to have the job of this remodelling. I don't like it.'

'Agnes Lonsdyke comes from a very old family–' his mother began, rather pink and annoyed.

'Lady Lonsdyke isn't suitable. She's taken on the job because she's a bored old woman and wants amusement. She's too gay, she hasn't had any children of her own, she's just as likely to get bored with the experiment half-way through–'

But Lady Lonsdyke didn't get bored with the experiment. Right to the end, she was absorbed in Joanna, and admitted grimly to herself that she dreaded the time when they would go back to England, and she would undoubtedly lose the girl.

'She chafes at anything that looks at all like a leash,' she wrote from Algiers to Mary Fenton. 'Heaven help any man who is fool enough to marry her. She has a mania for keeping an escape hatch open, and she won't believe me when I tell her that some things, such as marriage and parenthood, for instance, have no escape hatch.'

'How does *she* know?' William snorted angrily, when his mother showed him the letter.

'She's been married three times,' his mother said, indignantly.

'Oh, yes, I recall what happened to the last effort. Then she's no right to tell Joanna that marriage has no escape hatch, when she made one for her own marriage!'

'Don't get so worked up, William. Joanna won't listen to anything dear Agnes says, so why worry?'

'That's all you know about her, Mother. She may pretend not to listen, but she soaks everything up. She's afraid of missing something. She doesn't know much, she had no education—'

Mary Fenton wrote to Lady Lonsdyke, in Italy: 'Be an angel and extend the tour. Do anything in your power to keep Joanna out of England until I can arrange something between William and that nice Lavinia Durrance. While Joanna is not of age, I'm afraid my William is, and it isn't going to be easy.'

William wrote to Joanna, several times, but he received no answer. He shrugged, smiling, as he recalled that Joanna would probably be far too excited to bother about sitting down with a pen in her hand, but this idea was rudely shattered when Lady

154

Lonsdyke wrote from Sydney, where she had flown in desperation.

'It really is too bad. Joanna has been keeping correspondence with those awful people in London, and keeping them *au fait* with our movements. I thought I would make a change of plan and fly here, only to find that that Wetherall man got here the same day. She must have known about it all the time. My dear, he stowed away to get here, and there was an awful scene, and he was wanted by the police. He's due for a year, or something. Joanna calmly told me that he had "a stretch" coming to him. She wanted me to pay his bail, I think, with the idea of taking up her old friendship with him. I was so angry, I could hardly find words to frame my refusal. I think I shall bring her home at once.'

Mary Fenton wrote back: 'I'm cabling the cost of the bail, and enough to provide for any extravagances Joanna may incur, but whatever happens, dearest Agnes, don't bring her home. I'll stand any expense to keep her out there, and if this man has such a deep attraction for her, encourage it, don't try and stamp it out.'

William didn't see that letter. He was away at the time. But Elaine did see it. Mrs Fenton had no alternative but to let her read it, since she had heard her aunt arranging for the cable over the telephone.

'Oh, yes, we must encourage this,' Elaine approved.

'You think so, dear?'

'Darling Aunt Mary, there's nothing I'd love more than to see that odious creature come a cropper. William's potty over her, and it's so bad for him.'

'How far involved does the term "potty" indicate?' her aunt wanted to know.

'She's under his skin,' Elaine said, lightly, but her eyes were filled with the dislike she had felt for Joanna the first time she had seen her.

'Why don't you like her, my dear?'

'Do you?' Elaine countered.

'If it weren't for my son, and his unfortunate attraction for the girl, I'm afraid I should find myself liking Joanna very much. She has a way with her that I find very hard to resist. But she isn't for William. No, no, that would be tragic.'

'She isn't our kind,' Elaine said, viciously. 'She's got to be kept out. Why did Lady Lonsdyke take her and give her all that luxury? It'll be hopeless!'

'I thought it might be a good thing, while William and Lavinia—'

Elaine met her aunt's eyes.

'Elaine, dear, I suppose Lavinia *does* like William enough to—'

'Oh, Lavinia's quite potty over him, but she's inclined to show it, I think. I've advised her, but she just hasn't got what it takes to make a man hanker.'

'Darling, your vocabulary is deplorable!' Mrs Fenton protested. 'Oh, if only Lavinia and William would—'

'Yes, if only they would!' Elaine said suddenly. 'Then I could go home again.'

'Do you want to, dear?'

'Well, there was some thought about an interesting job wasn't there, and then the café burnt down. William just can't put his mind to raking up another antique for me to go into business, while his mind's on that wretched girl! So I might as well go home and marry Tom O'Keefe.'

'But my dear, I didn't know you were engaged!'

'I'm not,' Elaine said, shrugging an impatient shoulder. 'I was bored and bored and bored, and Tom's so stupid. Oh, he'd marry me to-morrow, if I were to say yes, and he's rolling in money, and the parents would like that. I thought it'd be rather fun to come over here, and work in one of the family businesses. Thought it would be exciting.'

'And hasn't it been? Well, interesting, if not exciting?' Mrs Fenton asked, anxiety in her eyes.

Elaine smiled and patted her hand. 'I think it might have been fun, if that wretched girl hadn't come, and turned William's head. As it is, the whole thing has been rather Joanna-ized, don't you think?'

Garry Wetherall was the first of Joanna's friends to see her since that Boxing Night, when she had come back from Pevensey House. He knew Sydney. He had been there as a boy, when he had worked the big ships. There was nothing thrilling about it. It was one of the big harbours of the world, and their police were no less efficient than the police anywhere else. He stared at Joanna, and the sour look in his eyes deepened. Hunger, and then that old gleam of excitement, in turn chased the sour look away.

'Get into the light, and let's see what they've done to you,' he said, moving to take her by the arms.

She shifted herself, quickly, lightly, just beyond his reach, so that a nearby hanging lamp shed its light on her, and made the diamonds at her ear lobes and throat glitter with a thousand slanting lights. The sea-green gown, almost washed out of colour, was of a stiffish silk, and lights chased all over it as she moved. Her hands, he remembered, had never looked so soft, so well-groomed, or so still.

He noticed her movement, and laughed thickly, under his breath. 'Forgotten what it felt like for me to touch you, and don't want to remember, eh, Joanna?'

She asked coolly: 'Why did you come here, Garry?'

He shrugged. 'The gardens of your hotel seemed about the safest place, honey. For a lot of things.'

He was a little put out by that cool stare. The last time he had been with her, she had seemed possessed of a craving, and he had kissed her, and that hadn't stilled the craving. He knew women. He thought he knew her still, although she'd been changed so much in the course of a year.

'They've let your hair grow,' he grumbled, 'and they've altered your voice. All cold. No feeling. Mighty correct but dull. That's what happens when they make a lady out of a nice girl.'

'Anything else?' she asked softly.

'Thanks for the bail. I suppose you fixed that?'

'I didn't. I wouldn't have, even if I'd been able to. Don't you know who did?'

He coloured angrily. He recalled that he was still in the rough clothes he had stowed away in, and he felt savagely that he would like to crush her, and all the expensive things they had put on her, to him, and to soil her, so that their work and her over-powering satisfaction in the result, was all spoiled. He wanted to spoil her so badly that he was sure she could see it, in his eyes, naked there, for all to see.

She smiled faintly. 'Ah, I see that you don't know, and don't particularly care. Well, I must go now. I wish you luck, Garry.'

'Just a minute,' he said, roughly, putting a hard detaining hand on her arm.

'Well?' she asked again, in that cool and unfamiliar voice which he instinctively hated. She glanced significantly down at his hand on her arm, and without quite knowing why, he removed it. When he had last seen her, she would not have acted like that. She would have tried to fling off his hand, struggled with him, spat and shouted, and afforded him a great deal of amusement, so that in the end he would have pulled her roughly to him and kissed her, and she would have finished up by straining that eager young body of hers to him, and both of them, spent, would have fought no more.

He laughed softly. 'O.K. kid. If you want it that way. But remember what I said to you, that first time we went out together. It's you and me for always. And the memory of me'll spoil anything new you try out. I see that you haven't fixed up anything permanent yet. Perhaps you've found out already that it's the truth, what I said about you and me.'

He stared at the bare third finger of her left hand, and turning on his heel, swung off again into the darkness.

Joanna went back through the trees, to the

hotel, anger searing her, her heart throbbing painfully.

'It isn't true. They haven't made a lady of me,' she whispered to herself. 'They've only poured something over me, that makes me look like one. I don't feel like one, inside.'

She wondered what Garry would have said, if he could have realized how much she had wanted him to kiss her. Habit dies hard. She was behaving in the way Lady Lonsdyke had taught her to, for every one of three hundred days. With each dawn she had had to listen to instructions. What to say and what to avoid saying. How to walk, to talk, to even look. A look could speak volumes, she had had dinned into her. She had also learnt the importance of just ignoring things. Of not looking, of not hearing, and above all, of not answering. To Joanna, who had been hot of speech and action, it had been learned the hard way. She couldn't break the new habits she had striven so hard to learn, in a matter of five minutes.

From Sydney, they flew to Rio de Janeiro, before going on to Washington and New York. Joanna liked the warmth and colour of South America, until Lady Lonsdyke tried to make a successful match for her. And then the beauty of it all was spoiled.

'Darling, you mustn't foist me off on to that nice young man,' Joanna admonished mildly. 'He's aristocracy, and you know what

I am. That's cheating, you know.'

'Rubbish, my dear. He's rich and idle and bored, and he wants to marry you. He's approached me about it already.'

'Nevertheless, you mustn't do it,' Joanna smiled. 'You should have made Garry Wetherall a present of me, if you wanted to throw me away so badly. I'm about poor Garry's level, and I think you know it. But poor Juan doesn't, and you'll take good care he doesn't.'

'You're not to tell him, Joanna! I absolutely forbid you to tell him!'

'It's no use getting angry with me. I shan't quarrel back. You've trained me not to. But you can't stop me telling the truth if I've a mind to. It's my antecedents I shall be discussing, not yours.'

'You really are a most tiresome, ungrateful girl!' Lady Lonsdyke protested. 'I've done all this for you, and you won't even allow me to bring it to a successful–'

'Dénouement?' Joanna murmured, smiling impudently. 'Ah, but I shall. When we get back to England, I shall ensnare William Fenton,' and she watched and was rewarded by the tiniest look of alarm in Lady Lonsdyke's eyes.

'No? Wrong dénouement? Ah, well, you can't expect me to learn everything in so short a time, can you?'

And so, in New York, Joanna contrived to

get to the forefront of the party when the photograph was being taken, when up till that moment, she had carried out Lady Lonsdyke's instructions to keep well back out of sight.

William stared hungrily at the photograph, the first he had seen since Joanna went away. She was smiling, but to him, she hasn't changed much. It was the same old tantalizing smile. The only thing that was different about her was that she carried herself as if she had nothing to fear. The old air of being on the defensive had gone. Hers was the earth.

Elaine made disparaging remarks about it, and his mother was frankly upset, but he heard none of those things. He was just seeing Joanna in that new setting, with the old short wild mop of curls gone, and the new softly waving hair which reached to her shoulders, giving her a new gentle, almost gracious look, which didn't go with the smile. He wondered what sort of person she was now, or whether they hadn't been able to change her.

Joanna wrote to him soon afterwards. 'William dear,' she began, persuasively, 'I've been so wrong. I should have answered your kind letters, but I was angry and hurt. I thought your dear mother and her friend had been plotting to keep me out of England. But now I see how unjust that was.

Your mother paid my friend Garry's bail, and that was most kind, wasn't it? And dear Lady Lonsdyke gave me the opportunity of becoming a rich rancher's wife, and that was kind too, and it shows that they have my interests at heart. So I know that they would want my friends helped, now that I am so far away. I cannot worry your dear mother, but you, I know, will help me. Won't you? It's poor Pixie. She married Alec after all, but Alec got into trouble with Garry's crowd and now it's rather a tiresome mess, and I can't do anything. Will you, William? (Or should I say *Bill?*)'

She posted it quickly, before she could alter her mind about it. When it had gone, she was wretched.

She danced with a man about William's height, at an Embassy ball. His hair was the same light brown shade, crisply wavy, just like William's, and he had the same level grey eyes. They called him Rick, and Lady Lonsdyke had said, before taking Joanna to the ball, 'If you won't consent to be Juan's wife, at least consider the young man I introduce you to to-night. You must marry money, child, or I can do nothing more for you. We go back to England in six weeks, and I really can't be bothered with you any longer.'

'How funny,' Joanna had mused, as she had wriggled into the lavender taffeta ball dress with its tiny sprigs of violets embroidered all over it. 'I thought you liked me for myself, and wanted me for a companion.'

Her wicked dark eyes met Lady Lonsdyke's in the mirror, as the maid wrestled with hooks and eyes and a stiffened petticoat. Lady Lonsdyke almost snorted, as she restrained her face from slipping into that unwilling smile of appreciation which Joanna could almost always call up.

'It isn't enough to like a person for herself, in this wicked world,' she said severely. 'One must have assets, too, and know how to show gratitude for favours received.'

Rick danced in silence for some time, and then he said suddenly: 'What are you *like*, Joanna?'

'Oh, you have to know me a little while, and then find out, you know,' she told him, her eyes dancing.

'I think if I knew you a lifetime, I'd never know, unless you told me,' he answered gravely. 'Besides, there isn't a lifetime. I have a fortune and I have to marry, because of my career, and your patron has introduced you to me.'

'Pretty stuffy, all this arranging, don't you think?' she chuckled. Then, suddenly serious, she said: 'I'm aching to tell someone, in return for an honest opinion, so I'll chance you, Rick. I'm a very unhappy person, because of a special problem.'

'I know that,' he said.

'Do you know what the problem is, Rick?'

'I think you're in love with someone, back home. Am I right?'

'No, Rick. You're so wrong. The problem is far more deep-seated. You see, my early life taught me to fight and spit and scratch and behave like a normal healthy animal. To do what I wanted, and behave naturally. Now I can't do that and it's a pity. You see, the trouble is, my body wants one man, and my heart wants another. What would you say to that, Rick?'

'I'd plump for the one your heart wanted,' he said, without batting an eyelid. She got the impression that he thought she was trying to shock him, and he wasn't going to play.

'But then, where would you come in, Rick?'

'Ah, well, d'you see, I've discovered it's a fallacy that life is short. Folks say so, but it's not so. Therefore, I work on a long-term policy. I'm glad to know your heart's taken, because it lets me out. You're a nice girl, and I wouldn't want to be the cause of making you unhappy.'

'Someone will, if you don't,' she told him, lightly.

'How come?' he wanted to know.

'This is the end of a world tour, you know. I've met many people as well as seen many places. So many people you meet, have a lot of wise things to say. But none of them seem to meet my case. You see, the man I love, won't ever marry me. There's a mother, who schemes, and a girl who'll make him a Good Wife (and I won't!), and then there's the man who makes me all upset and wanting things I can't find.'

'You'll have to sort it out yourself,' Rick told her.

'I haven't got the right equipment to sort it out. Bill could, if he had that sort of problem, only he hasn't. I've got the problem, and I'm always searching, but life didn't give me the sort of start which would enable me to thrash things out.'

'If you ask me,' Rick told her, 'it's you who had the right start, if all you told me about your early life is true.'

'What did I tell you?' she asked sharply, and taking him literally.

'A good deal more than you meant to, honey,' he said smiling. 'Don't worry. I won't pass it on. Only remember the old tag. I don't know where it came from. A poem, I guess. I can't remember. "Though it comes with storm and strife, no other heart will do." I guess you were made for battle and thunder, honey.'

CHAPTER SEVEN

It was springtime when Joanna came back to William's county. It was as lovely as he had said it would be. Lady Lonsdyke said, as they neared St Christopher's, the austere stone mansion that had been in her family for generations, 'I'm being very weak about all this, Joanna. I said I was going to cast you loose if you didn't please me by marrying yourself off well. And now look at me. Bringing you back here to be a menace to everyone! You're a witch, girl, that's what you are!'

'Never mind. I'll soon make myself scarce, now I'm in England,' Joanna comforted absently, her eyes raking the hedges, the little farmhouses, everywhere where there was a scrap of pearly blossom and fresh green. 'It's all so lovely here,' she sighed.

'You really think you'll like it, Joanna? It'll be deadly dull for you, you know!'

'I think this is what I always wanted,' Joanna marvelled, half to herself, and remembered poignantly that one mad Christmas she had spent with William. 'What did Mrs Fenton do last Christmas?' she asked suddenly.

'Do you really mean Mrs Fenton, or her son?' Lady Lonsdyke asked sharply.

'We were in Mexico,' Joanna frowned. 'I don't think I recall hearing what they did. I asked, because they had such a dull Christmas at home the year before. They could have such fun, with such a lot of money.'

'What would you do, in their place, for that very doubtful season of the year?' Lady Lonsdyke scoffed.

Joanna was not to be drawn. She said, instead: 'How long may I stay with you?'

'How long do you want to stay? It's up to you, unless, of course, you make a nuisance of yourself.'

'Let me stay until I'm twenty-one,' Joanna said impulsively. 'You can put up with me for five weeks, can't you?'

'Yes, that's a very good idea. I'll launch you with a coming-of-age party. But you really must decide on someone then, my dear. It's the last effort I shall make on your behalf.'

'Oh, I don't want any more parties,' Joanna said, impatiently. 'I was just thinking of a suitable time to clear out. Besides, it'll give me five weeks to get a job. You see, before you did things to me, I could get a job in less than five days but now it will have to be something rather different,' and she smiled that slow tantalizing smile which no one could resist.

'Well, if that's how you feel, my dear,' Lady Lonsdyke said, looking anxiously up at her home as the car swept round the curve of the drive, 'I'm sure I can manage one or two useful contacts for you. I hardly like to let you loose in London again, or heaven knows what mischief you'll be up to.'

Joanna didn't answer to that. In her handbag was a letter which she had received from William Fenton. A very brief, hardly friendly letter, she mused, as she went over the few lines again, those lines which she had memorized. She supposed that he was furious with her for making him run about for those friends of hers. She wondered how Pixie had treated him, and whether Alec had been grateful for the services of William's expensive lawyers, and whether they all realized that it was at her instigation that help of any kind had come to them. She missed the hurt which was underlying William's few words.

Lady Lonsdyke swept into St Christopher's and in less than no time was organizing everything, examining her enormous mail and sorting invitations, as well as presiding over tea in the old dark library. Joanna wondered why these people always took tea in the library, and glared resentfully at the dogs, remembering that other library, where she had first met Lavinia Durrance.

Almost as if Lady Lonsdyke were reading her thoughts, she said suddenly: 'Here's your first party, my dear. An engagement party. I always like Lavinia Durrance.'

'Who's decided to have her?' Joanna asked lightly, in that new tone which robbed the words of any rudeness or belligerence.

Lady Lonsdyke covertly watched her, as she said: 'William Fenton, apparently.'

Part of Lady Lonsdyke's training had ensured that Joanna could hear the most startling news without giving anything away. She continued to stare absently out of the window on to the close-cropped turf of an ornamental garden, where early blossoms were being gently shaken from nearby trees to lie like large blobs of fluffy snow on the young green. Even her hands were still. Lady Lonsdyke decided regretfully that Joanna was too apt a pupil, and went on, purposefully: 'You'll have to wear that last new gown I bought for you. The brown velvet with the beige roses and the beige pleated underskirt. You shall borrow my topaz set, if you like. Yes, I think you will look very nice in that. *Joanna!* You're not listening to me, child.'

Joanna turned with a slow smile, and an impudent grin in her eyes. At least, it seemed to lurk in her eyes, for nowhere else in the correctness of her face could it be said to be. And yet Lady Lonsdyke felt that somehow the girl was managing to laugh at her.

'I was just thinking how nice it would be to wear my old camel coat and the plastic shoulder-bag, and to thumb a lift in a lorry on the Great North Road,' she said, sauntering out of the room.

Lady Lonsdyke telephoned Mary Fenton almost at once. 'It isn't any use, my dear. I'm frantic. Just when I think I've managed to control her nicely, she breaks out, and then I don't know where I am. No, it's nothing one can put a finger on, and yet I feel she's just cocked a snook at me. I shall be quite glad when you see her, to tell me what you think of the result of my experiment. How is William?'

'The tiresome boy doesn't show any pleasure at all in his engagement. I did as you asked, and sent you an invitation for Joanna, but really, I'd much rather she didn't come. Can't you manage it somehow? Keep her away–'

'No, dear, that simply isn't possible. We don't want her to think it's engineered.'

'She thinks that already. In fact, she wrote to William and told him so, and it almost set him against me!'

'I didn't know that! When did she write?'

'She wrote before you left America. Since then, he's been rushing about getting some of her East End friends out of trouble. She asked him to! Really, Agnes, it *is* too bad!'

'She's sly. No, no, I don't think that's true,' she hastily corrected herself. 'Oh, drat the girl, I just can't help liking her, but most of the time I could shake her. It isn't really that she's underhand in the way she does things. It's just that she doesn't bother to announce what she's doing, and one is apt to forget that she's likely to do anything. She looks so bland, so – so *un*energetic! Oh, dear, she's the first person who's made me feel really inadequate, and you know me, Mary. I just won't admit defeat.'

'Are you keeping her with you?' Mary Fenton asked anxiously.

'I don't know. I've promised to launch her with a coming-of-age party. It's the least I can do.'

'What did you hope to do, when you first took her up?'

'My dear, I hardly know, at this stage. I think I was bored and hoped for something interesting to come out of my experiment, but nothing I expected has happened. At least that awful Wetherall man seemed to fade out of the picture.'

'I wish he hadn't,' Mary Fenton said fervently. 'Why don't you take him up, do something for him, so that it pleases Joanna? She might marry him.'

'You're too hopeful, my dear. I'm only very happy to think you got William engaged to

Lavinia, or I can't think what might have happened. I'll explain that later, when I see you.'

'Well, thank heavens William won't see her until the party,' Mary Fenton said, evidently too distracted to take in that last muttered sentence of her friend's.

But William did see Joanna before the party. He saw her at an auction of the barn in which he had been interested. Joanna, fresh and lovely in a pea green suit edged with soft brown fur, smiled coolly across at him and for a time outbid him until she grew tired of it. At first he didn't recognize her, and when he did, he sat open-mouthed and forgot to watch the proceedings, until he found that the barn was his at a far higher price than he had intended to pay.

'Well, if you want a thing badly enough, Bill,' she murmured, coolly shaking hands with him, 'you must keep on plugging at it!'

'Joanna! What did you do that for?' he demanded furiously.

'Wasn't it worth it? It must have been, for you to be interested after all this time. Eighteen months, isn't it?'

'Here, let's get out of here. Who are you with?'

'No one. I borrowed Lady Lonsdyke's second-best two-seater, and drove myself. Oh, yes, I'm accomplished. I can even stay on a horse for about five minutes. Can I drive you somewhere?'

'I have my own car, thanks,' he said shortly.

'You're as rude as I used to be,' she observed, pulling on her gloves, 'but I didn't know any better.'

'Where are you going now, Joanna?'

She shrugged. 'To find some lunch somewhere, I suppose.'

'Take lunch with me, Joanna. I've such lots to say to you. What are you looking for?'

'Lavinia,' she said, curving her mouth impishly at him.

'She isn't here,' he said flushing.

'I haven't offered my congratulations, yet, have I? Nor my thanks for your helping my friends. It was kind of you.'

'Joanna, look, do we have to be so formal? Come on, let's leave Lady Lonsdyke's car here. They'll look after it. Come over to the Red Lion with me. Remember?'

'Oh, yes. I remember this village. Christmas Day. I saw that tiresome fellow, the one who thought he recognized me then. I stared right at him, but he didn't seem to think he knew me to-day. Odd, isn't it, what a car and a few glad-rags will do?'

'Don't be bitter. It isn't that. You've changed so much yourself, Joanna. I wish you hadn't.'

'Why should you care one way or the other?' she asked, falling into step beside

175

him, across the cobbled square. 'You should be interested only in Lavinia.'

'Damn Lavinia,' he muttered.

'Do you know, I should hardly have suspected this of you, Bill. Your integrity always stuck out a mile and hit me in the eye,' she said, inelegantly, but with something reminiscent of her old manner, which made him look sharply at her.

He settled her in a corner seat, near one of the bottle-glass windows, and didn't answer that one. He looked thinner, and not very happy, she considered.

'Your last letter wasn't very friendly,' she observed. 'Didn't you like helping me?'

'I didn't want to help you,' he said morosely. 'I wanted you.'

It was said in an undertone. Their eyes met suddenly, and he said, in a fierce undertone which only she could hear: 'For heaven's sake, Joanna, can't you see? The minute you left this country, I saw what had been wrong all the time, and it was too late. Too late! I didn't know until then that I was in love with you. And I still am! Don't you see?'

She whitened, but still stared at him, as if she couldn't tear her eyes away.

'Stop that,' she said at last, in the same fierce undertone. 'Of course it wasn't too late. I could have come back. I would have come back, if only you'd said. I'm that sort of fool. But you didn't say. You just kept on writing nice friendly little notes, with a hint of your mother's patronizing in them. Let's keep in touch with the child, lend a friendly hand while they're licking her into shape! That was all! That's why I never bothered to answer them. They didn't deserve an answer. But it's too late now, and you had no right to say anything about it.'

'You mean you love me, too?' he whispered.

The soup came, and the tension snapped. They both sat back, and felt distinctly relieved. It was all so mad, this kind of conversation, in the dining-room of the inn in that village which had meant so much unhappiness for them the last time they had been together. Joanna wished passionately that she hadn't succumbed to the impulse and gone to see his barn. William found himself wishing that he hadn't decided, after all, to buy the thing. It was all too tied up with a great deal of the misery he had suffered since then. In a sense it had been self-flaying which had led him to do it. Before he went to the auction, he had gone through his old nannie's village, called for a moment in the little church, and then driven on, madly, insanely retracing their steps eighteen months ago, and it had hurt just as much as the memories of it had hurt.

When the waitress had gone, they stared dumbly at each other and began mechanically to eat. Nothing more was said during the meal, until he selected a wine.

'Joanna, let's drink to – its being – not too late?' he pleaded.

'Don't be absurd,' she said shortly. 'It's not only too late. It's dead. All of it.'

She saw him wince. 'Well, I had to hurt you. I'd like to go on hurting you. You do things so correctly, and you miss the bus every time. And all the things they've done to me, trying to make a lady out of me, have just aggravated the situation. If they'd only left me alone–'

He waited, breathlessly.

'I'd have gone back to Garry, and stayed with him,' she finished, mercilessly. 'Let's drink to a future where neither you nor I will behave quite so crazily as we have done. Where we'll have the sense to put a few safe miles between us.'

'No,' he said huskily. 'We won't drink to the future at all. We'll drink to – the rest of to-day. Come, Joanna, you can't deny me that. I'm not engaged yet, and you *are* by way of being an old friend now.'

She closed her eyes, and slowly nodded. Everything in her prompted her to say no. No, we can't even spend an hour together, alone. It isn't right. But she didn't.

She watched him garage the Lonsdyke car, and arrange to pick it up later that day, and then he unlocked his own and she got in beside him. They drove in silence for a little while, through the lovely countryside, until they came to the beginning of a wood. The road ahead narrowed and curved through the green twilight, lonely and mysterious. William pulled up, and said curtly: 'Let's walk. There's something I want to show you.'

She followed him, single file, through a path which steadily narrowed, and the trees grew more dense. Finally they went through a gully, up some rough steps made by hewn pieces of tree trunk, and out into a little clearing, where a stream ran down some rocks. In the centre was an ancient well.

'A wishing well,' he muttered. 'I used to come here, and throw a stone down. Yes, I was reduced to that.'

'What for?' she asked, in scarcely above a whisper.

'For you to come back to me,' he said, staring down hungrily at her. Suddenly he swept her into his arms, and she found herself clinging to him, crying, and muttering that she loved him. He was saying incoherent things, too, which sounded very much the same as her own murmurings, and then they were both quiet, as his lips came down on hers.

A long time afterwards, he tilted her head back, and wiped the tear-tracks with gentle fingers. 'They said you were marrying some chap in Rio,' he said thickly.

She shook her head, biting hard on her bottom lip.

'Then some chap in New York.'

Again she shook her head.

'You never seemed safe,' he added.

'I wrote to you,' she gasped.

'I know,' he said, grinning tautly, and she thought with amazement that it just wasn't possible that William, self-possessed William, could be so moved.

'And you kept throwing stones in there, Bill?'

He nodded.

'What happened? Did you get fed-up? Lavinia, I mean.'

He ducked his head and pressed his face hard against hers. She put her hand up to it, but he took it in his own, and held on to it.

'Joanna! Little Jo, I can't let you go again. Can't help it, but someone'll have to fix it about Lavinia. They're good at fixing things for everyone else. Jo, come away with me. Let's run away, now, and get married. We could get married in a matter of hours. Jo, let's?'

'You never called me Jo before,' she muttered, succumbing to his kisses again, and thinking, with an upset feeling, that he could make her world rock even more than Garry Wetherall could, and with more lasting effects.

'Jo? Will you?'

'Bill, I can't think straight while you're holding me. Let me go. Yes, let me go, while I think. It isn't right, dear. Nothing is right about it. Don't try to talk me down. Bill, I'm me – Joanna, who isn't anybody at all. No one wants me. They've groomed me to look like a pretend-lady, but I'm still the same Jo underneath. Darling, darling Bill, I can't marry you! I should want children, and it wouldn't be right if I were the mother of your children. You know it wouldn't be. Besides, you *are* practically engaged, and you didn't have to be, if you hadn't wanted to. Bill, listen to me–'

'I never wanted anything, only you, from that first moment when I found you in the snow. I've just been harried by my family, and the only wrong thing I did was to let them manage my life. Jo, dear, I want you – isn't that enough foundation for a happy life together? I don't love Lavinia. She knows that. We've even talked about it. I think she even knows how I feel about you, but she just doesn't care. She said so. On that basis, does it matter, does anything matter, except that the two people who marry are the ones who both love each other?'

'You're talking me out of it, out of the right conclusion. I can't come to the right conclusion without a lot of effort, and you know that, and it isn't fair. Oh, Bill, it isn't fair.'

'Jo, will you, dear? Will you?'

He bent and kissed her again, and ran his lips all over her face and her closed eyelids. She let herself slide under the avalanche of his passion, and nodded. Weakly she told herself that she was being horribly wrong about it all, but she couldn't do anything about it now.

She didn't remember much of the walk back through the gully to the car, nor of William starting it up. She was conscious of the greenness of it all, the lovely heart-lifting fresh greenness of it all. She felt light-headed, and dare not look at William.

After a little while, she said: 'Where are we going?'

He chuckled. 'Let's be really romantic. We'll have to resort to the really mundane special licence business for speed, but first, let's find the tiniest, most wonderful little church, and fix a blessing service with the vicar. I bet no one's thought of that yet. Where shall it be?'

'Do you have to drive so fast, William?' she asked, nervously. 'It isn't like you, and these roads are so narrow.'

'It isn't like you to be nervous, Jo, either,' he said, looking sideways at her, but he did slow down a little.

'Bill, I wish–'

'Yes, dearest?'

'I wish you'd telephone your mother first.

And Lavinia. And I'll phone Lady Lonsdyke.'

'And have all the hounds on our trail, to stop us?' he asked, indignantly, and then started laughing. 'Darling, I thought you'd be gloriously reckless with me!'

'That's just what I'm not, at this moment,' she muttered. 'Bill, there's something about all this – oh, I don't know. I want it and want it and want it, but somehow, I feel horribly uneasy. Perhaps it's because I feel we aren't doing the thing–'

'In the conventional way? My dear, they've had their meddling hands on you too long. That was one of the things I first loved about you. You saw what you wanted, and you went all out to get it–'

'Trampling whoever was in my way,' she said, in amazement, with wide eyes. 'I don't want to trample anyone, in order to be your wife, Bill.'

'You won't be trampling anyone,' he said, with the faintest hint of impatience. 'They'll fix a suitable marriage for Lavinia and she'll forget about it and be happy, and so shall we.'

'But she might not forget so easily, Bill.'

He swung into a wider road and let out again, and she watched the speed needle in agony. 'Not Lavinia. She hasn't got that much depth in her to worry very long. Besides, she's afraid of losing her looks. No, my dear, she'll be all right. If anyone, it's my mother who'll be unhappy, but I'm afraid she must learn that she's been possessive and managing for too long.'

'You don't love her any more, Bill?'

'Yes, of course I love my mother.'

'Will she ever love me?'

'That's a question I'm not prepared to answer now, my dear, and I don't care very much. She'll like you, she'll be charming to you, and I think you'll have to be satisfied with that. But I love you, with all my heart, and–'

'Oh, Bill, look out! That lorry! It's–'

'My God!' he shouted, wrenching at the wheel. 'He's not going to stop. He's–' and the last thing before the crash which Joanna remembered, was a kind of scream coming from Bill's throat, and what sounded like– 'Jo, my dear, I *can't*–'

CHAPTER EIGHT

Joanna came to in a ditch. Blood was all over her, and the source of the pain revealed that blood was still flowing. Her head felt as if it were bursting, and her legs wouldn't work.

She staggered to her feet and stood uncertainly. The quiet country road, with the secondary road on which the lorry was travelling, slanting sharply up to it, were still deserted. Only the lorry, which had finally come to rest at an angle against a telegraph pole, was in sight. Through a mist which turned out to be creeping blood from her own wound, she saw what appeared to be a body half hanging out of the driver's cabin. It wasn't very clear because the windscreen of the lorry was splintered too much to be seen through. A great star-shaped hole sent radiations of cracked glass all over it. Steam came out of the radiator, and liquid was flowing from underneath. Of William and his car there was no sign.

She gingerly moved forward and went reeling down on to the road. Somewhere, somehow, there was help, and she must get it. Behind the lorry, as she worked round it, a gaping hole torn in the hedge, came into view. Four wheels still turned slightly, and with a lurch of her heart, she saw that it was the car, upside down, in a field which lay lower than the road.

'Help,' she muttered. 'Must get help.'

Hours later, it seemed, after stumbling along interminable miles, she found herself on a hard horsehair couch in a tiny room, and homely voices talking quietly round her. Then there was the clang of an ambulance bell. That made everything suddenly all right, and she stopped fighting against the engulfing darkness. There was no need to struggle any longer.

When she awoke again, she was in an unfamiliar iron bed with white coverings, in a long ward in which thirty-nine other similar beds were ranged side by side. Someone lifted her a little and put a feeding cup to her lips, but no-one offered information or asked her for any.

When at last she did ask where she was, she was told that she was in a hospital in Bedford.

She stared blankly, and even forgot the ugly throbbing of her forehead.

'Is that where we were when the crash happened?' she gasped.

'Oh, no. You were brought here because we happened to be less crowded.'

'What happened to–' Joanna began.

'The other two people were taken to a hospital nearer the crash, but that one was rather crowded. You're not too badly hurt. We'll have you out of here in a few days. Now, Sister will want some information, so if you feel up to giving us your name and one or two other things–'

'Don't you know my name?' Joanna frowned.

The nurse smiled. 'Unfortunately, you had no identification on you.'

'But my handbag. Where is it?'

'Now, don't worry. Perhaps it was still in the car, in which case the other hospital will know more about it. How did you come to be so far away from it all?'

Joanna strove to think. 'I must have been flung clear. I don't know. I was all covered in blood, and I tried to get help. I can't remember much about it.'

'Well, never mind that now. Let me have your name and address, so that we can notify your people.'

Joanna raised startled eyes to the nurse. She was plain and efficient and sensible, and there was a practical kindness about her which made it difficult to assess just how far she would go, to help anyone, without exceeding her duty. The thing was to find out what had happened. To discover if anyone had inquired about her, and if they knew what she and William had been about to do. On that hung everything.

Joanna tried again. 'I'll give you all those details in a minute. But first, what happened to – the man who was driving the car? I suppose you don't know?'

'Indeed I do,' the nurse said. 'He was taken to the nearest unit for X-ray and immediate operation. Now you, on the other hand, had a most wonderful escape. Just a cut on the forehead. Oh, yes, it bled quite a lot, but that's nothing to worry about. You should be very thankful you came out of it so well.'

'How do you know about the other people in the accident, if they didn't come here?'

'It's in the newspapers,' the nurse said, her pencil poised.

Joanna shut her eyes. Of course, they would have identified William, because of his pocketbook and the papers he carried, and the fact that the car was his. He was well-known in the district. He would naturally be in the papers. And that meant that his mother, and Elaine, and Lavinia, and Lady Lonsdyke, and the detestable Dr Charles Lindsay, would all know about it. Probably they were all round his bedside, at this very moment.

She choked down the rush of tears, and bit hard on her lip. William would be all right. They'd all see to that. What she had to do was to concentrate on keeping her name out of it. He wouldn't want them to know, until he was able to deal with the situation.

To keep her mind off the sound of that last screamed-out remark of his, as the lorry had rushed at them, she tried to remember what had happened to her handbag. It was imperative that she should know, and that no one else should. It had been a small suede pull-up bag. With a tremendous effort, she recalled that the handles were on her wrist, the little bag lying in her lap. If she had been thrown out, the chances were that it was lying somewhere in the rank tangle of grass and weed, in that stinking ditch she had crawled out of.

She decided that she'd have to go and look, when she got out of here. 'Mary Smith,' she muttered, indistinctly, choosing the first name that shot into her head. 'And I haven't any people.'

'Your address?' the nurse asked, writing busily.

'Just changing jobs,' she said. 'Resident post.'

'Your last employer?' the nurse pressed.

'No. That's all finished. I'll be all right,' Joanna said, and closed her eyes purposefully.

Nevertheless, although the hospital authorities seemed satisfied with those few particulars, they were not satisfied with her condition, and she was still in bed, heavily bandaged, a fortnight later, when a man detached himself from the insurging crowd of visitors, and walked purposefully over to her bedside.

She raised enormous dark-ringed eyes to his and then closed them again. 'What do *you* want?' she asked, sourly.

Dr Lindsay laughed softly, and sat in the chair by her bedside. 'They told me you'd changed,' he offered, 'but I find you pretty much the same. What do you call yourself this time?'

'Don't you know?'

'Haven't the foggiest,' he said cheerfully, 'so I played safe and asked to see the lady passenger in the accident, who I understood had been brought here. I also smiled nicely at the nurse, and here I am.'

'Well, you can take yourself off again,' she muttered.

'Now, listen, Joanna,' he said, dropping the bantering tone. 'I've come to help you.'

'Who sent you? Mrs Fenton?'

'No. Lady Lonsdyke, as a matter of fact.'

Joanna stared at him for a moment, and then at the nurse, who brought in a vase of daffodils, tulips and narcissus, and put it on Joanna's locker.

'It's high time you had a visitor, young lady,' she remarked, briskly, looking pleased.

'Did Lady Lonsdyke send those?' Joanna muttered, when they were alone again.

'No. They were my idea. Must be pretty mouldy for anyone as active as you, to be a prisoner like this.'

'Prisoner!' she whispered, her eyes enormous. 'Just what did you come here for?'

'To see if I could help you.'

'What's wrong with me? They'd tell you, wouldn't they?'

He nodded. 'They would. And they have. I'll tell you afterwards. Lady Lonsdyke sent me, to find out if you'd see her.'

'Why?'

'She thinks you were just running away again.'

'And you think I wasn't!'

'Joanna, don't stall with me,' he said earnestly. 'I'm your friend, this time. Not against you at all. You were with William.'

'Did he say so?'

Dr Lindsay didn't answer for a moment, and then he said: 'Well, no. Poor old William isn't fit to say (or think) anything.'

He watched her, and waited. Even he wasn't prepared for the effect he achieved. Her face crumpled, and she turned her head sharply away, thrusting her arm across her mouth to try and still her crying.

'Here, here, you can't do that, Joanna. This is a public ward. That, by the way, is another thing Lady Lonsdyke wanted fixing. She hates the thought of your being among all the others. You'd like a private

191

room, wouldn't you?'

'What for?' she flashed, turning a ravaged face to him. 'They all keep saying there's nothing wrong with me, just a cut. What do I want with a private room, with just a cut head?'

'It went pretty deeply. They're not sure just what damage has been done. You're to stay here under observation.'

She looked horrified at him for a second, and then a hopeless look came into her eyes, which hurt him in some unaccountable way.

'William's dead, isn't he?' she said flatly.

'No. Good Lord, no! He's in pretty poor shape, and won't be about again for a long, long time, but he'll be all right.'

'Who said so?' she jeered, without much enthusiasm.

'He'll be all right, I *think*,' Charles Lindsay said, carefully. 'Remember, I'm his friend. It's as much to me as to anyone, that he'll have a chance of recovering.'

'Do they all know I was with him?'

'No one knows,' he said slowly. 'Lady Lonsdyke guessed, because of her car that you borrowed, without even telling her. When it was found, someone offered the information that you'd been driving it, that William had got it garaged to be picked up later, and that you'd both gone off together. Only Lady Lonsdyke and I know that, Joanna.'

'Why doesn't his mother know?'

'We thought we wouldn't tell her, Lady Lonsdyke and I, until we heard what you had to say about it.'

'Where is William? Still in hospital?'

'No. He's been shifted to a private nursing home. You weren't thinking of trying to see him, were you?'

'With his doting mother and fiancée hanging around? What sort of a fool do you take me for?'

'They keep telling me they've made a little lady of you,' he smiled, with raised eyebrows.

'Tell Lady Lonsdyke she's been wasting her time. I just don't want to make the effort any more. It was fun while it lasted, but I'm not striving to be polite to you. You're no friend of mine.'

'I would be, if you'd let me,' he said, leaning forward.

'The other visitors are going. Hadn't you better tag along?' she fumed.

'Not me. I'm privileged. I only came in with them to catch you on the hop. I knew you'd refuse to see me if I came at any other time. Now listen to me, Joanna. Lady Lonsdyke guesses what was going on, and she says you're to come to her. You may not have any finer feelings for her, Joanna, but she's very fond of you. She's spent a good deal of money, time and effort on you–'

'For her own amusement,' Joanna put in.

'And for your ultimate gain,' he added. 'And now, when you're alone and friendless, and ill, she isn't kicking you out, as I would do in her position. She wants you back, to nurse back to health again.'

'What sort of cut have I got? Where is it?' Joanna asked suddenly.

He traced an imaginary line right across the length of her forehead.

'Is it – will it show?' she asked, suddenly frightened.

He nodded, slowly, purposefully. 'But possibly not so much if you're good, and stay here.'

'Was – was William hurt – on his head?' she whispered.

'His back, and his legs,' Dr Lindsay said, after a moment.

'Anything else?'

'He might not walk again,' he said.

She caught her breath and shut her eyes. Presently, she said: 'When he's – well enough to ask – if he does – about me, will you say I'm all right? Not tell him about my head? Just say I'm all right?'

'Why, Joanna? Wouldn't you rather see him yourself?'

'Holding his mother's hand, I suppose!' she flashed back.

He smiled, unwillingly. 'All right, I admit his mother's not likely to let him have any

194

visitors for a long time. Any use asking if you'd like to send him a note, via me?'

'What's wrong with the post?' she asked, in a surly tone.

'They may shift him to somewhere else. Like me to keep you in touch, Joanna?'

She thought about it, and shook her head. 'No. Listen, Dr Lindsay, would you tell me the truth, if I asked you something terribly important?'

'I daresay,' he said, unwillingly.

'Well, what does Lady Lonsdyke think I was – we were–'

He eyed her for some minutes, and then he took her hand, in a firm grip. 'She's more fond of William than she is of you, my dear, if that's possible, and the one thing which she doesn't want to see, is you two young people messing your lives up. Do you understand me?'

She shifted impatiently. 'What would happen to me if I got up and walked about? Or went out?'

He got up, frustrated, not knowing quite what he had hoped to achieve, and filled with a sense of failing two people very near to him.

'You wouldn't drop down dead, if that's what you want to know!' he said shortly.

'And you hope I would!' she grinned impudently up at him. 'Tell Lady Lonsdyke from me, "Remember what I said about my old camel coat." She'll know what I mean.'

He repeated it, looking mystified, and rather irritable. 'Can't you send a rational message, if you're going to?'

'Oh, but that *is* rational!' she said mockingly, for the first time using the cool well-bred little voice which had caused Lady Lonsdyke so much effort, and given her so much pride in her handiwork. 'It's entirely explanatory, also, and above all, it shows her that my health is not as poor as you'd have me believe!'

Lady Lonsdyke shifted impatiently.

'Oh, if only I hadn't got this wretched chill, and had to stay in bed, I'd have gone myself, Charles! How tiresome of you to have managed nothing more than that!'

'What else could you have done?' he asked, with a lift of the eyebrow.

'I don't think I'd have antagonized her. I was just beginning to understand that child a little. Tell me, do you think she really cares for William Fenton?'

He nodded. 'I think she does.'

'I can't believe they were going away together.'

'I think they were just out for the day, frankly.'

'It isn't *like* William!'

He smiled ruefully. 'You don't say that it isn't like Joanna, I notice!'

'Oh, that mad child would do anything that came into her head, without considering the consequences. He hasn't asked for her yet, I suppose?'

He rubbed the back of his head.

'Well, he certainly hasn't asked for Lavinia!' he said dryly.

'Charles, it isn't any use. You must get her moved out of that awful ward for me. Ring up the hospital this very instant. Make whatever arrangements are necessary. Never mind whether she consents or not. She isn't twenty-one yet, remember!'

'All right,' he agreed.

He wasn't gone very long. When he came back, Lady Lonsdyke knew that something was very wrong.

'She's cleared out. Left a note discharging herself,' he frowned.

'What arrant nonsense, Charles! It takes two legs to get out of a place, and two legs that are good enough to walk. Why, she hasn't been out of bed since the accident!'

'That isn't so,' he said, furious with himself. 'She's actually been making little necessary trips up the corridor. She asked me what would happen if she walked very far, went out, in fact, and instead of telling her what would happen, I just said something damned silly about not falling down dead!'

'Oh, Charles, there are times when–'

'I know, I know, but who'd think a patient in hospital would have half a chance to get out!'

'But how *did* she get out?'

He remembered uncomfortably that he had used the word 'prisoner'. 'She wandered to the bathroom, saw an open door with someone's overcoat behind it, and as her ward was on the first floor, anyway, I imagine the rest was easy. It wouldn't be easy to you or me, I suppose, but stowing in a laundry van or some such thing would be child's play to Joanna.'

'But her bandaged head!'

'A porter says he remembers a girl in a darkish coat, with a head-scarf that may or may not have been a check duster. Part of the kitchen staff sleep out, so he didn't think another word about it. Where would she go, d'you suppose?'

'How far *could* she go, in that condition?'

He looked thoughtful. 'I imagine that being Joanna, and extremely tough, she could get quite a long way. But how far she'd get after she saw what remained of her forehead, is another question.'

CHAPTER NINE

High summer on the Great North Road meant the combined smells of the blistering heat on the tarmac, the rank smell of petrol fumes, the oily smell of chips frying, and the over-powering odour of hot cocoa. Sounds whittled down to the screech of brakes as cars and lorries pulled in sharply to avoid a crash, and the dull lumbering sound of the eternal traffic pounding by.

Joanna stared out of Alec's place, and wondered how long she could stand it. Pixie, with her one-time brassy smartness gone, her young body spreading to fat, and her face innocent of make-up, served lorry drivers with eternal cups of tea, tarts with shredded coconut on top, and snacks, all of which had its own special smell. Joanna stood at the chip frying apparatus, turning scrubbed potatoes into the required long shapes under the cutter which went Cr-ump-Cr-ump! with a monotony which set her teeth on edge. Alec, in greasy shirt sleeves, leaned somewhere and watched her. All the time, he watched her.

One evening, after it had been teeming with warm rain all day long, Pixie came into the tiny box of a room which they had given her, three months ago, and sat on the edge of her camp bed, staring at her.

'Turning in early, ducks? Don't blame you. Early night never did anyone any harm.'

'Did you want me, Pixie?'

'Well, in a way, I did, come to think of it. I just wondered if you knew, well, friend to friend, as you might say, when the door comes open sudden and a draught stirs your fringe—'

'Does it show?' Joanna gasped, clasping a hand to her forehead.

Pixie nodded. 'I thought you'd like to know, ducks. No one else has seen it yet,' she added, rather futilely. 'Well, now, why don't you keep a bit of pink plaster over it, then if your fringe does take a flying leap upwards, it won't show so much, eh?'

'Thanks,' Joanna muttered.

'There's another thing. The men got talking to-night. Not very loud, see, but I never let on I heard 'em, and it struck me that the bloke they was talking about, the one what was fixing a job for to-morrow night, might be a mutual friend of ours, if you take my meaning!'

'Garry?' Joanna muttered, the old fear leaping into her eyes.

'Not that you need worry about it, duck, seeing as you don't see the chap no more these days. Still, I thought you'd like to know. He's in the money, and there's only one way he can make that much money–'

'How do you know?' Joanna said fiercely. 'He might have caught on to a way of making it honestly or–'

'Or he might have won a football pool, or his old auntie might have snuffed out and left him the family jools–' Pixie scoffed.

Joanna decided that either Pixie had coarsened a lot since she had married Alec, or the grooming which she herself had received had spoiled what had been a one-time very real friendship. She gave up the problem. Thinking made her head ache.

'There's another thing. (Got a lot to talk to you about to-night, haven't I, kid?) Seems we're going to have a Little Stranger. Oh, no, don't get soppy, dear. It's just one of those things. Well, you know how it is–'

'I *am* very happy for you, Pixie,' Joanna insisted, and added swiftly, 'and you'll want this room, of course. You haven't got so much room, after all, and I've been very grateful for it.'

'That's what I always say about you. You catch on so quick,' Pixie told her. 'What will you do? Go back to Auntie's?'

'No, I don't think so. Can you give me a week or two to look round? Perhaps I'll need only a day or two. Anyway, I'll be out all day, looking for something.'

Pixie's eyes narrowed for a second, and then her face regained its old easy camaraderie. She was relieved. She knows about Alec, Joanna thought, fuming inside her. She's seen him looking at me, all the day, every day. Heavens, why did it have to be like this?

She lay on her back, staring at the lights on the ceiling, long after Pixie had gone. Since she had left Lady Lonsdyke's, she had made the unpleasant discovery that the past eighteen months had spoiled her for this sort of life. She hated the squalor of it, and people noticed, and wouldn't give her any peace.

She didn't want to go back to her old friendship with Garry Wetherall. In these last three months, she had strenuously fought against it. Each time she had seen him she had given a different reason why she felt different. And all the time the gleam in his eyes had left her feeling that her resistance was leaving her. She recalled the old feeling, the old uneasiness and the old excitement. Eighteen months of Lady Lonsdyke's had not taken away all those memories. She remembered the gate-crashing of parties, the stolen rides, the madness and the sweetness of it all, and wondered what sort of person she could have been then, to enjoy it. She remembered too poignantly that last meeting with William, and didn't know how she would be able to be with Garry for even a little while, without showing that the old enchantment had gone.

Subconsciously she was waiting to hear from William, or of him. Both Charles Lindsay and Lady Lonsdyke knew Pixie's old address, and it wasn't a very difficult guess that she would go back to Pixie. Mrs Adey would be only too willing to tell them where she was, if they had bothered to inquire at Cedars Street. Joanna didn't know how William was. Each day was a stretch of hours spent in dissuading herself from telephoning, to try and find out. She would rehearse the telephone call, pretending to be all sorts of different and improbable people (never herself, they would never tell *her* how he was, she was certain!) but someone's secretary or housekeeper, inquiring on behalf of a friend or a business acquaintance. Always she gave up the idea, telling herself that she'd never be able to disguise her voice.

There was the faintest sound at the door. There was no lock or bolt, but instinct rather than reason always drove her to pull a chest in front of it, or fix a chair beneath the handle. She had automatically taken this precaution after Pixie had gone out. Now she watched in fascination as the tarnished knob rattled gently. That would be Alec, trying to get in. He had never done that before.

Suddenly she started to laugh, soundlessly. No wonder Pixie hadn't wanted to make a fuss about the coming baby! There was no baby coming. It was just the only way that Pixie knew how to throw Joanna out of her home, without severing what had been a very long friendship.

Joanna felt a flood of pity for Pixie. There was no earthly reason why she should care for Alec so much, but she did. She loved him blindly, and almost obstinately. She must have known, before she married him, what he was like. She could afford to throw friends away because of him.

Joanna didn't wait to get another job. She packed her few things the next day, and said a quiet good-bye to Pixie.

'Where will you go, kid?' Pixie asked, curiously, and almost afraid to hear the answer.

'Never mind. You won't like hearing, anyway,' Joanna said, trying to call up the old grin without much success.

She took a bus back to Cedars Street, but was told that Garry now had a place of his own. A nice little flat over a shop, a bus-ride away. Joanna asked if she might stay there for the time being, and left her luggage.

Garry wasn't in, but the woman said he would be back soon, and let her wait for him. Joanna sat on the black horsehair sofa, and reflected that this room looked rather like the one she had come to in, covered in blood, after the accident. The home of the village policeman. This sitting-room of Garry's had just the same unlived-in look. It was, she realized, just an accommodation address. A bolt-hole. She couldn't imagine where else he lived. Probably somewhere like Mrs Adey's.

And then Garry was there, at the door.

He hadn't expected her. Perhaps he hadn't even seen the woman downstairs and so didn't know anyone was waiting in his rooms.

It was heart-warming to see the look which leapt into his eyes, on sight of her. It was a long time since she had felt *wanted* by anyone.

He grunted, after he had recovered himself, and came in, kicking the door shut behind him.

'What's the idea?'

'Garry, the last time we met, you said we could be as we were. Remember?'

'What if I did?'

'Without strings, you said, Garry.'

'I'm not that much of a mug, Jo.'

'What strings, Garry?' she whispered, feeling very tired.

He started to laugh. 'Call yourself sophisticated,' he jeered. 'I'd never ask *that* sort of string. Not from you, kid, anyway. From you,' he said, a rough edge coming into his voice, 'I'd want something special.'

'What, Garry?'

'I'd want a guarantee that you weren't still hankering for young Rockefeller.'

She shook her head miserably. 'I don't know how I can give that sort of guarantee. Except to say it was like an illness, and one gets *over* an illness...'

She stared at him, and then on inspiration, moved into the strong light. 'I haven't seen or heard of him since I got ... this,' and with a sudden sweep, she pushed her heavy hair off her forehead, and revealed the scar. It was purple, angry and livid in spots. It zigzagged across her forehead, and gave her eyes an angry look. She watched his face, and saw the familiar horror spread over it. She was used to that look, when the wind blew her hair back, or when she was hot, and pushed it back herself, without thinking.

And then Garry was across the room, pulling her roughly to him. 'So that's what made you cut clear and come back. You damned little fool, why didn't you tell me before? Jo, why didn't you tell me?'

'What good would it have done, Garry?' she muttered, her face pressed hard by his hand, against the roughness of his jacket.

'Think I can't do anything?' he muttered, his lips against her hair, so that she hardly heard what he said. 'I suppose young Rockefeller didn't want to dip his hand into his pocket any more. Well, what I've got may be easy come, easy go, but I'm not tight-fisted with it. Like I said, kid, I'd spoil any other romance in your life, while I was breathing, and here you are, you see, back again, here where you belong.'

Joanna closed her eyes, and whispered inaudibly, 'Bill, I'm sorry, darling, but there's nothing else left.'

'Isn't it, kid? Isn't it so?' Garry persisted.

'Yes, Garry, I've come back,' she choked.

CHAPTER TEN

Black Rock Bay was on a part of the coast entirely new to Joanna. Garry played his master-stroke here.

'You've got to get some sea air, after all you've been through, honey,' he had said, positively. 'A car accident's enough, but a session of old Max is just a bit much on top of it all.'

'Doesn't it show a bit, Garry?' Joanna asked, nervously, touching the new bandages on her forehead.

'Just you wait till we get those stitches out, and then we'll see,' he had promised.

London was hot and airless, and Joanna chafed against the second attempt to iron out that dreadful scar across her forehead. Finally, at the end of August, Garry had taken her out of the heat, the dust and the petrol fumes, and driven her to this unfrequented patch of coastline.

'Where will we stay?' she had asked, faintly, as she stared with misgiving at the jagged black rocks and the sand so white that it almost dazzled like mirror glare in the sunshine.

'In a cottage in a hollow – it's sheltered,

and you can get down to the beach in no time down a gap in the cliffs. I'll show you.'

'Where are the trippers?'

He laughed till he ached. 'Kid, you won't get trippers here. Isn't that what you want? A bit of peace?'

'Fancy *you* liking a quiet place, Garry!'

He shifted uncomfortably. 'Well, I've got a bit of business in these parts, see, kid, and I can kill one bird with two stones. Do my bit of business, and get you rested up and well. Then we'll go the pace, eh? Back to the old tempo?'

Mrs Bird, the little old woman who lived in the cottage, was tremendously thrilled.

'Is your wife not well, then, sir?' she wanted to know.

'This is my sister,' Garry said, firmly, before Joanna could speak. 'She's had an operation, and she's got to rest. The best of everything, now, and here's something on account.'

He got out a packed wallet, and Joanna – who was used to Garry and his way of doing things – felt her mouth opening at the wad of notes in it. She looked away quickly, as she saw the old woman stare at the notes and up again at Garry.

'Appendicitis, was it, then, sir?' she breathed, counting the notes, and almost kissing them, Joanna felt.

'No, it wasn't,' Garry said testily. Then he

decided to be a little grand, and he swept back Joanna's fringe. 'See that? There was a long scar there. She's had it taken out. Plastic surgery, they call it! Costs the earth. She's got to have rest.'

'Oh, aye, that little old plastic business, I know all about that,' the old woman said, settling down to familiar ground. 'My son, he got bashed about like in one of they submarines and they did rare wonderful things to his face. A sight he did look, but now it's all right. Wonderful men, they are. What was the name of your man, now? Would it be the same?'

Joanna felt sick, and wished Garry had said nothing.

Garry, however, was very angry. 'My sister didn't go into hospital!' he snorted. 'She had a private man. Come to our house. World-famous, he is!'

The old woman was unconvinced. 'My son, he'd know him, if you was to say the name. My son, he's rare interested. Says there be only three top-liners in the business. He'd know 'n if he was all that famous. Makes a study of it, he's that pleased with what they did to 'n.'

'What's your son do for a living?' Garry asked, suddenly switching the subject. Joanna breathed again, as he turned the old woman's conversation away from that dangerous subject, but later on, she was to

210

realize that it wasn't just cleverness on Garry's part, but a genuine desire to know, occurring at that moment. That it achieved the other purpose was sheer good luck for them both.

'Coastguard, he is,' the old woman said, proudly, and Garry, after a short silence, started to laugh.

'I don't see aught to laugh at, sir,' she said frowning.

'Bless your heart, I wasn't laughing at your son,' Garry said, bursting into loud laughter again. Joanna noticed the helpless quality in the laughter, as Garry said, going out of the cottage, 'I was just having a good laugh at myself.'

If Garry struck the old cottager as not being quite the type of gentleman she had imagined, Joanna filled the old woman's idea of what a young lady should be like. In self-defence, Joanna had resorted to the old manner which she had learnt with Lady Lonsdyke. She sat dreaming into the golden air of late summer, and the old woman's remarks and artless questions slid right over her head, seldom getting an answer.

'You seemily in love, miss, I do suppose,' was a question to which Joanna didn't bat an eyelid, but it came and was repeated several times. The old woman had a great deal of kindliness, and knew of the love affairs, the births, marriages and deaths for miles around. She had been servant at the big house, local midwife, taken a hand with the boats, and knew everything that was happening in the district.

'How old are you, Mrs Bird?' Joanna asked her in some amusement, one day, watching the old woman making pastry with deft hands, at the little old-fashioned oven.

'Seventy,' Mrs Bird said, with composure.

'What has life taught you?'

Mrs Bird looked startled. 'You're mighty young to be wanting the answer to a question like that, miss. Why, I'd say it'd taught me to do what I knew was right, and to hold me head up and to fear naught. No matter what discomforts doing right'd bring me, never mind. I could look any man in the face, see, and no one to say me nay.'

Joanna found that rather involved at first, until it tied up with what William had said, in those few sweet days when he had first known her, and they had wrangled and parted. A slow flush came up over her pale face. She thought, I can't look anyone in the face. That's what he meant. Anything to get on top, that's me, but I can't look anyone in the face.

'Like your brother,' Mrs Bird said suddenly. 'Now there's a young man as has found a place in my old heart. Not yet a week you've both been here, and I couldn't say no to him, no, not by a long chalk.'

'Couldn't you really?' Joanna murmured, leaning forward.

'No, that I couldn't, nor I wouldn't want to. Look at him. As straight a look as any young man ever had. And so kind and devoted to you, miss. I like to see a brother look after his sister.'

'Your son doesn't like him,' Joanna reminded her, as she thought with a smile of the burly young coastguard who came up to his mother's cottage twice a week, and scowled at the visitors as if he'd like to see them flung over the cliff-top into the sea. 'He doesn't like me, either.'

'That's because you're so like the young wife he lost,' the old woman said. 'Isaac, he took it bad like. So bad, he went right on living in Kitty's mother's cottage, where he is to this day. Died in childbed, she did, and my boy never got over it.'

'I see,' Joanna whispered. 'Perhaps he feels you shouldn't have London people with you. You see, our ways aren't your ways. I can't see why you have us, since you're, well, rather simple in your way of living.'

Mrs Bird said hardily: 'Because I walk upright, don't mean to say as I can't walk with nor touch them as don't. That isn't the way the preacher says to be, and I mind what he says most sincere, miss.'

'You mean that if you like people, it doesn't matter what they are, or what they do, you'd still go on liking them for them-selves?'

'And why not?' Mrs Bird demanded. 'Isn't that what young Mr Starr tells us from that pulpit every Sunday? Miss, you should go down there, you really should. Maybe last Sunday you wasn't up to it, but you'll go this week?'

'Oh, I will,' Joanna said suddenly. 'Oh, I will!'

Mrs Bird looked at her sharply, as she straightened up from the oven. 'Why, miss, what ails you? You're crying? Is it aught I said, as has upset you?'

Joanna shook her head. 'Are you making some tea, by any chance?'

'I will, right away,' Mrs Bird said, and when she poured out the sweet steaming liquid, Joanna said:

'Don't tell anyone. I hadn't meant to think of it any more. It's just … well, I remem-bered the last time I went into a church.'

'That would be before your accident, miss?'

'It would be a rather long time ago,' Jo-anna mused. 'Two years. Two years is a long time. I was with someone I loved.'

'Lor, miss, is he dead?'

'I don't know. Sometimes I think so. They won't tell me. I can't find out, and now it's so long ago, I'm almost afraid to try.'

'Ask your brother to. He wouldn't want to

214

know you were unhappy, and holding it to yourself like a load fit to break your back. Open your heart to him, miss.'

Joanna stared, her jaw dropping, and then she started laughing as Garry had, that first day when Mrs Bird had said that her son was a coastguard.

'Miss, you're ill, that's what it is! I knew it! I knew it all the time. I'd best call in the doctor.'

'No. This time it'd be a proper doctor, and I think that would shatter me. Oh, you think I'm raving, don't you? But I'm not. Garry's not my brother, and he'd raise Cain if he thought I was still thinking about someone else. Don't look like that – you haven't perjured your soul harbouring us here. He only wants to marry me. That's all. Mrs Bird, my virtue is all I have. It's blazing white, the only thing I have to my credit. I have not anticipated marriage with Garry or anyone else, so don't look so upset. I just have to stay with him. He's all I have left. Even I can't bear the thought of being alone.'

She stared out over the shimmering sea and the cliff-edge. 'Do you know, there was a time when I didn't care. Life was a high adventure, and I just squared my shoulders ready to meet what came. But now, I've bashed my head against the wall too often. I'm a little cowed, I think. For the present, perhaps. One day I'll fight again.'

'I think you ought to be in bed, with blankets, seemily, and a hot brick,' Mrs Bird said grimly. 'Where is your ... brother?'

Joanna's lips twitched. 'Oh, didn't you believe me?' she asked, reproachfully.

'Believing's one thing. Acting as you mean to go on is another. He said he was your brother, and I think you've said a good many things you hadn't a mind to, miss, when you weren't yourself, and which you'll be sorry for, maybe to-morrow. But don't worry. It won't go no further.'

Garry came into her bedroom at sundown, leaving her door open as he usually did, and ostentatiously knocking first.

'What's wrong with the old girl?' he muttered, after he had made loud inquiries as to her state of health.

'What *is* wrong with her?' Joanna asked carefully.

'Said she thought I ought to stay in with you more, and talk to you. Honey, it isn't talking we want, is it?'

'Garry, I've said I'm grateful for the plastic surgery. I've said I'll stand by you, whatever business you happen to be conducting, and help you if you want me, and ask no questions. I can't – repeat *can't* – do more, and I never gave you to expect I would.'

He scowled down at her.

'Just what *are* you up to, Garry?'

'I'm buying a boat,' he said, smiling

broadly. 'A fast, trim, beautiful little craft. Guess who went with me to advise me? The old girl's white-headed boy, in between coast-guarding. How's that for a laugh?'

Joanna sat up. 'Her son ... *went with you?* To buy a *boat?*'

He nodded, still grinning. 'Now, be a good girl, and don't ask any more questions, and you won't make your head ache worrying.'

'Garry, damn your boat. What I want to know is something quite different. Who is old Max, who operated on me? I mean, is he a *real* doctor? All above board?'

'Not satisfied?' Garry asked sharply. 'Any pain?'

'No, no. No pain. Quite comfortable. It just occurred to me, you acted so strangely when Mrs Bird asked you his name. And it's so expensive, and if you did all that for me–'

'Yes?' he asked.

'Well, I'd just not be able to repay you, and that would–'

The gleam died out of his eyes as he saw what she meant. 'Honey, in this wicked world chaps like me don't pay in hard cash. It's really a most complicated barter system. Now, be a good girl and shut up that beautiful mouth of yours, before you ask a Pandora question. Remember that dame Pandora?'

He nodded, and went out.

Joanna lay back, eyes closed, slow tears

pushing their way through. Before she had met William, all this would have been highly exciting. Now, with William's way of thinking, and Lady Lonsdyke's showing her a peep into a different world, she had no stomach for all this shoddiness, this hole and corner way of living. The sun had lost its brightness, and the sea its brilliant blue. The cottage wasn't fun any more, but a sort of prison. She could force her way out of it, she knew, but there was only one way out, and that lay through London, inevitably to Cedars Street and the Great North Road.

Mrs Bird brought her up a light supper on a tray and stood looking at her as she ate it.

'You don't have to wait, miss, till Sunday betimes, if you was wanting to see our young Mr Starr,' she said obscurely.

Joanna looked slowly up at her. 'Yes, I haven't been out yet, have I? That's a very good idea.'

The church belonging to Black Rock Bay shared its clergy with Holcombe Sands, the next hamlet, but the present clergyman lived in the white stone house at the end of Black Rock Bay. Joanna walked slowly down there from the cliffs the next day, and was very thankful that Garry took himself off for so many hours.

'Mr Starr's over at the church,' Joanna was told, and reluctantly she had to go across the churchyard and into a church that was oddly reminiscent of the one in William's nannie's village.

She hesitated outside for too long, and was almost going away, when someone said, 'Wouldn't you like to come in and see what it's like, before you go?' and she turned to find a young man staring at her, who was at first sight so much like William Fenton that she couldn't tear her eyes away.

And then she saw that he wasn't really like William. His eyes were a kindly light brown, and patient, but he was William's height, and his hair, light brown, was, like William's, the type which wouldn't lie down when brushed.

She nodded, because she couldn't speak, and walked into the church beside him.

'You're Mrs Bird's new visitor, aren't you?'

Joanna shrivelled at the kindness in his voice, and wanted to run from the tone in it, which suggested that he was reaching out spiritually and touching her.

'She's talked about me?' she asked roughly.

'Only about your accident. She's a good woman. She never had a daughter, and lost her only daughter-in-law.'

'Yes. She told me. It's funny. How people remind you of those you've lost. Her son can't bear the sight of me, because – and I can't bear the sight of you, for the same reason.'

'After an accident,' Arthur Starr said mildly, 'one's values tend to become distorted. I find that this place is a wonderful help to me, in sorting things out.'

'*You* need to sort things out?'

'I do indeed. I think that my experience in that direction is so wide, that I might be of some help to you,' and his lips twitched a little.

She noticed. 'That's how Bill used to smile at me, as if he could see I was in a muddle, but he loved me for it.' She averted her eyes, and said sharply: 'And you can see I'm in a muddle, and it amuses you, doesn't it?'

'Yes. I can see myself. Only no one helped me to sort myself out, until one day a kindly old man with white hair and the most amazing blue eyes, invited me to come into church, and talk it out of my system. I pass on the advice as excellent, and a swift cure.'

Joanna sat in a pew beside him, and sat looking at her hands. 'Of course,' she said suddenly, 'if Bill's dead, there isn't any need for me to unload. It doesn't much matter what I do or what becomes of me.'

'On the other hand,' Arthur Starr argued, 'if he's alive and is ever told of that remark, what d'you suppose he'd say?'

Joanna nodded agreement, flushing. 'Still, either way, it doesn't matter. You see, there's a match-making mother, and he's probably too ill to care much what she does for him.

He obviously doesn't care about me any more. They knew (at least, friends of his knew) that I came out of it looking like a Horror. I never heard any more – from any of them. If I'd known he was disfigured, it wouldn't have made any difference. I'd have asked after him.'

'As it was, did you?'

She shook her head. 'As if anyone'd tell me!'

'Someone might have, who didn't know you. You didn't even try,' he commented.

Stung, she was telling him the whole story before she realized how far she had committed herself, and then it didn't seem to matter very much. Because it was so briefly, and yet so emotionally told, she gave him a graphic picture of her life, from the Rorton days, to the present, sparing nothing.

'We were to have been blessed in some little church,' she finished, but she was now beyond tears. 'Do you know, that nice little Mrs Bird is quite happy about me, just because I have assured her I'm not living in sin with Garry Wetherall. That, I consider, is not a lot worse than some of the things I have done, or half-done or thought about doing. It's right, you know, the way it's turned out. I shouldn't have made Bill happy.'

'Would you like me to make inquiries about him? I mean, you'd like to know how he was, wouldn't you?' Arthur Starr persuaded.

'No,' Joanna said at last. 'Perhaps I'd better let sleeping dogs lie. He might be alive and married to Lavinia and–'

'And of course, he might be a hopeless cripple or horribly disfigured, beyond, say, the hope of the plastic surgeon, and that wouldn't be very pleasant, either. I see your point.'

'I didn't mean that,' Joanna said fiercely. 'D'you think I'd care? D'you think I'd *care*?'

'Then it should be all quite simple,' was the mild reply.

'No, no, no! It isn't simple at all. Don't you see? He doesn't see my way at all. He said I'd got a twisted way of thinking, through being with people like that. My friends, you know. He didn't want me to go back to them.' She made the effort to be coherent, and went on again: 'He won't understand why I went back to Pixie and Alec, when I could have stayed with Lady Lonsdyke. He won't understand why I went back to Garry, even though it meant getting rid of the scar. He'd think I ought to have kept the scar, rather than go back to Garry.'

'But you don't agree. That being the case, you see no harm in being on Garry's side even now. Now he's, shall we say, invested in a rather curious form of amusement?'

'You mean the boat?' she whispered. 'Anyone can buy a boat, and anyway, Mrs Bird's son's helping him choose it.'

'No, I don't mean the boat,' the quiet voice went on. 'I have to talk to all sorts of people, and I know people. I know the sort of people I've seen Wetherall with, and I know what they're doing. And from what you tell me of the young man, I think you've got a good idea of what he's doing, too.'

CHAPTER ELEVEN

Garry seemed surprised to find that Joanna had gone out on her own so suddenly.

'You feeling up to it, kid?'

'Of course,' she said, regarding him warily. 'Why?'

He assessed her, and said slowly: 'It was only Max's opinion of course, but he felt you ought to take it easy for a bit. Only go out with someone else in tow.'

'Why?' she asked, alarm sharpening her voice.

His eyes slid away from hers.

'Garry, he *was* a proper – I mean, he *did* know what he was doing, didn't he?'

'He was a top-liner, in his own country. He happened to get mixed up with something, that's all. Sniffy lot, the medicos here. What's it matter what a chap's been doing on the side, so long as he knows how to cut people up? Got to make a living somehow, eh, kid?'

'If that's true,' Joanna began, slowly, fear rushing through her, and leaving her breathless. 'But then, why did he say I mustn't go out alone? It's only a skin operation, isn't it? He didn't mess about with any nerves or anything, did he?'

He took her into his arms, with the old charm, which in those far-off days had allayed all fears, if only for the time being. Watching him, and herself, she found with misgiving that the old charm didn't work. His little action merely heightened her suspicions.

'Don't worry, honey. Don't worry. Now do you think I'll let anyone mess you about?'

'You act clever sometimes, Garry, and it scares me.'

'So do you,' he said, calmly, letting her go. She recalled that he never pressed his attentions when he found she wasn't ready for them.

'How?'

'You discharged yourself from hospital when you were supposed to stay in there under observation. You took off the bandages but who said you could?'

She clapped a frightened hand to her mouth.

'Max gave it as his opinion that the damage had been done, at first. A little pressing from me in the right quarter, set him thinking that he might be able to fix something, and a bit more of the squeeze set him really working on it. But he wasn't happy. He said the whole thing had gone deep.'

She nodded, her eyes never leaving his face.

'All right, honey, that's the low-down.

Now will you stop worrying? All you have to do is take it easy. And think that when your hair blows back, no one will see a thing.'

'That's what you think,' she retorted, stung, and pushed back her hair, for the fun of seeing his face. Fun? Exquisite torture, she realized, as the familiar horror came into his eyes. 'You see? It only happens when I'm scared or overtired, and then you can see it. Not much, just a faint blue line, but it's there, and it's horrible. Isn't it? I think it's worse than the original scar. Don't you think so, Garry?'

She was conscious, as she waited for his answer, that everything went very still. The seagulls weren't screaming. The tide, which was going out fast, made only the faintest kissing lap-lap on the base of the big rocks. The bay, in which they stood, was deserted with a chill empty kind of look which, despite the blazing sunshine, made it all seem forlorn, desolate, unfrequented, and not quite wholesome. She shivered.

He shrugged, as if to push off some unwelcome thought. 'Oh, stop it, Joanna. You'll give me the creeps in a minute. Now you shut up worrying. We'll go back and make him have another go, and this time he'll get it right, or know the reason why!'

'No!' she said, her voice rising a little. 'No, no bungler's going to mess me about again! I feel, deep inside me, that if an expert had done the job, it would have been all right the first time. No, Garry, he isn't going to touch me again, and to tell you the truth, I don't quite feel so overcome with gratitude as I did at first!'

'Gratitude? What d'you mean?' he asked roughly.

'Gratitude,' she repeated carefully, 'was the feeling that was uppermost, when I promised to come back, and to stand by you. Oh, Garry, you must have known that. I looked on you as the one friend I had. There was no one else.'

'Well?'

'Well, I don't think it was a very friendly act to take me to someone like Max,' she murmured.

'What was I supposed to do, then? Look at that – that thing he removed, and keep telling myself you were as good to look at, as you used to be? I'm no saint, Joanna. I never pretended to be. I don't like the ugly things of life.'

'But you indulge in them!' she flashed.

'I meant women and dirt and poverty and grubbing every day at the same mean little under-paid job, like the fools of this world do! You know what I mean, Jo. As to what I'm indulging in, as you call it, you don't mind being bought things with the proceeds! Where d'you suppose the money's coming from, to pay old Mother Bird? Santa Claus?'

He caught her roughly to him again. 'Jo, everything in this life has to be paid for, I told you that before. You've made a make-shift out of me time and time again and you have to pay for that now. What happened in Sydney? Gave me the brush-off, didn't you? But I knew you'd come back, when you were ready. What happened when you got mixed up in the car smash? Back with young Rockefeller, weren't you? And you play the saint – that's a good one! I happen to know he was engaged to a cute little blonde who had been vetted by his mother, *but* ... where does that put you? Because I happen to know you knew about it too, at the time!'

She struggled to get free of his arms, but he held her too tightly. She closed her eyes. She could have said she was going to be married, but that would not only betray William, it would also infuriate Garry at this present moment, and in this ugly mood of his. She used the silent tactics taught by Lady Lonsdyke, and at the same time tried to think.

'Are you engaged in smuggling, Garry?' she murmured.

That had the effect of making him release her, and then he started to laugh.

'No, honey! The silly things you come out with. Of course I'm not smuggling. They don't do that nowadays.'

'Don't they?' she retorted. 'Then what

have you bought a boat for?'

'To go fishing at night, with our coast-guard friend!'

Alarm shot into her eyes. 'Garry, what are you thinking about? You wouldn't be going to harm him, would you?'

'Well, that's a funny thing to say to your boy-friend! Don't you care if he does me a mischief? Or have you gone mushy over him? I've seen you around with a tidy number of escorts since I've known you, honey.'

'What if I have?' she retorted sullenly.

'What you did when you were out of my hands was one thing,' he muttered, and didn't bother to finish his remark.

She was to remember that ugly little scene.

The hot spell lasted, and Garry, with his usual overpowering high spirits, chose to forget their quarrel, and took her out in the new boat, and drove her into the nearby towns for shopping. The coastline lower down was less forbidding, and there were still quite a number of trippers, piers which were illuminated at night, and scores of little boats coming out like a menacing fleet of the enemy. She laughed a little with the pleasure of seeing so many people frequenting the coast-line for a purpose that was obviously not sinister.

'Want to go dancing, kid, or don't you feel like it?'

She caught her breath, and shook her

head. 'That's just it, Garry. Since Max worked on me, I haven't any energy. I don't want to do anything. I'm not saying *that's* his fault, but it's worrying.'

'Take it easy, take it easy, honey,' Garry murmured absently, and didn't press the point about the dancing, any further.

He did say, however, that he considered a gentle swim might do her good, and fixed it for the next morning.

'Oh, no, it's Sunday,' she said involuntarily.

'So what?' he retorted, the old gleam in his eyes.

'I wanted to go to church,' she said, wondering why she should feel so embarrassed about telling Garry that.

First of all, he burst out laughing, and when he was tired out with laughing, he chose to get angry.

'I thought you'd taken the wrong turning, Ma Bird working on you,' he said fiercely, 'but now I see it's gone further than that. You've taken a header for the dog-collar, haven't you?'

'Don't be coarse about Mr Starr, Garry. I won't have that. He's a good friend, for anyone who'll have him. I haven't got so many friends that I can turn him down with comfort. After all, you hardly see me! You've left me stranded high and dry since I came here.'

'Yes. Yes, you've got something there, Jo,' he conceded, his anger dying as suddenly as it rose. 'But that's all different now, honey. I've almost finished the job I came to do.' He stared at her speculatively. 'Care to come fishing to-night? There's a moon.'

Cold fear clutched at her. 'There isn't a moon, Garry, and you know it. And what's special about to-night? You never mentioned it before.'

'I only asked you if you'd care to,' he said carelessly. 'You don't have to, if you don't want to. I just thought you might like to, because–'

'Because what?'

'Because you've been about as inquisitive about that boat of mine as any woman could be,' he said laughing.

'I don't care about the boat any more,' she said, listlessly. 'I don't care about anything.'

'Except me, kid.' He stopped the car, and stared out over the shimmering water below them. He didn't make the mistake of touching her this time, but just sat back easily, in a typical attitude of his, hands dangling as he rested his arms one over the back of the seat, the other over the wheel; a cigarette dangling from his lips. The old insolence was around his mouth, and a provoking look in his eyes. 'You still care for me.'

'Don't count on it, Garry,' she said, in a low tone.

'Well, there's no one else, kid. You said so yourself. And bear this in mind, too. You said that an expert could have done better for you than I did with old Max. Don't you believe it. All the experts breathing couldn't save young Rockefeller. You forgot that, when you flung my generosity in my teeth, didn't you?'

She jerked her chin up, her face whitening beneath the slowly forming tan. 'What did you say, Garry?'

He appeared surprised. 'But you know what happened to him, didn't you? I mean, it was in all the papers! Even I saw it, and I wasn't looking for it, so you must have seen it somewhere.'

'I didn't. You mean … he died?'

He shrugged, and it was far more convincing than if he had given a straight affirmative answer.

The whole lovely day was spoiled. Joanna could feel Garry watching her, his eyes mere slits, looking sideways. She did not question the truth of what he had implied. But she knew that he had stage-managed imparting the truth, so that it had occurred just then, when he was losing, and losing badly.

For a brief instant, she struggled. Fighting was still second nature to her. Energy, however, was the thing that was lacking now. Energy, and some inward urge, to make her want to resist Garry and all he stood for.

'What does it matter?' she breathed, at last, and she sensed rather than saw him slump back in his seat, immeasurable relief written all over him.

'That's just what I say, kid! What does it matter? What does anything matter? Ships that pass in the night, that's what we are, every man jack of us!'

He slewed further round in his seat, to face her squarely. 'Listen, honey, remember what I said that first time we went out together? You and me, all the way, to the end – whatever that may be! Well, I've no holes to pick in that arrangement. Have you?'

She shook her head slowly, hardly hearing him. So William, dear *Bill*, had died, on that wonderful day he was to have married her. Just like that. A candle snuffing out. With that knowledge came such a sense of finality that she was overwhelmed. It wasn't the same as the sense of loss she had felt all these months, since she had left the hospital. Always, at the back of her consciousness was the feeling that William was *there*, somewhere, and that until she saw the notices of his marriage to Lavinia, he was still free, still hers, Joanna's, and that there was still the possibility that he would ask for her, send for her. She never once entertained the idea of going herself, in person, and asking to see him. If she had found

233

thinking easy, she might have come at last to the important question: had he really meant to marry her that day, or had it been just a mad jaunt which he would have been regretful about, at a later date?

Now, all that had gone. Nothing was possible any more. William was dead. Her life had narrowed down suddenly, shut in with a snap like an accordion when the playing was done and over.

'Kid, are you listening?' Garry was insisting.

She turned dazed dark eyes on him. 'Yes, oh yes,' she said, mechanically. That was all Garry ever wanted. To claim her attention, so that he could talk to her.

'To-night, then?'

She had no idea what it was he had planned for to-night, beyond the fact that the boat was involved, but it was all one to her now. 'Yes, oh yes,' she said again, without much interest.

'Right. Come in warm things. We'll be out in mid-Channel, you know. Oh, and anything you wouldn't want to leave behind, just in case we had a mind to go further down the coast, shall we say? Bring along. Any little things, you know. Not a great pile of luggage, mind!'

'Luggage?' she asked dully. 'What for?'

'You're not listening, kid,' he said, laughing, and turned round to the wheel again.

'Treasures, little things, if you like. Things you'd want to keep with you, just in case we didn't come back.'

Garry stayed behind to put the car away, but Joanna got out and went straight up the steep path to the cottage. She went by habit, not looking where she was going, and twice stubbed her foot on a stone jutting out from the rockery which bordered the front path. Old Mrs Bird, watching from the window, said to her son, 'Dear life, what ails the lass? Looks like she's tooken a death blow, if I ever see one!'

Isaac came and stood beside his mother. He said so very little, but she was used to him. She could feel in his silence that she had his attention.

'A right pretty lass, and a right lonely lass,' she said, with insinuation.

'No, Mother,' he said firmly, thoroughly understanding her meaning. 'Fasten up a wild bird in a cage I never would!'

She nodded tiredly, and abandoned the idea. It was an attractive one, one dear to her own heart, and she believed, to her son's. He, too, had taken a blow, when he had first seen Joanna.

She opened the door, and took Joanna's arm.

'Come in, lass, do! What ails you, now? Where have you been all this long day?'

Joanna spoke slowly, as if she had

235

difficulty in mouthing the words. Her lips had a stiff look about them, and her eyes were glazed. 'Out in the car, with Garry.'

'Was it a nice run, now? Did you good, your cheeks all tanned, I declare!'

'Yes,' Joanna said, and stared at Isaac. If he hadn't been there, she might have unburdened her news to his mother, but she could never have given a confidence before that strange silent young man, with his haunted eyes and tight, bitter mouth.

'I'll give you a lacing of whisky in your tea,' old Mrs Bird said suddenly, getting up as she spoke. 'It's my belief you need it, my lass.'

Joanna nodded absently.

Isaac stood staring at her sombrely, and presently his gaze penetrated the thick fog which seemed to surround her mind, and she looked straight at him. 'Did you say something?' she asked.

'No, but that isn't to say I couldn't, if I wanted,' he answered, disconcertingly.

His mother said, 'Now, Isaac,' warningly, and he scowled.

'Drink this, my pretty, and it's an early night for you, by the looks of you. Been doing too much gadding about, that's my belief.'

'We're going fishing,' Joanna said, dully, as if she had learned the words by heart. 'Tonight.'

Isaac's head shot up, and he looked from Joanna to his mother.

'Well, now, I wouldn't, my dear, if I was you,' Mrs Bird said unhappily. 'Not to-night, lovey. Go when there's a moon, now, that's much the best.'

'To-night,' Joanna repeated. 'We're taking luggage, too.'

Isaac hauled himself to his feet. 'Don't go, miss,' he said, as he crossed the little room and went out. Even Joanna caught the warning in his tone, and she looked frightened.

Garry came in before she could talk to Mrs Bird, and he stared from one to the other for a moment before speaking.

'You don't look too good, Jo,' he said, concern in his voice. 'Make her take a nap before I come for her, Mrs Bird, there's a good soul. We're going down to Holcombe Sands to a show, and I thought it might add a touch of novelty if I took her by sea, in the new boat. Get a whiff of sea breezes before we go into a stuffy concert hall, eh, kid?'

And in that little speech, he made every-thing sound all right. Mrs Bird's face cleared, and she smiled reassuringly.

'That I will, sir, I'll do that for sure! She shall get right into bed for a nice long nap, and I'll get her up all bright and ready for you. Though I don't hold with her coming back late, now. But there, sir, you'll look after your sister, that I do know!'

Garry bent and brushed Joanna's cheek with his, and Mrs Bird nodded approval. But to Joanna, the little attention was a warning. *Don't tell them anything. That's my story – see that you stick to it.* It couldn't have been plainer if he had voiced the words for all to hear.

After he had gone out again, Joanna said urgently: 'I don't want to go to bed. I want to see Mr Starr. Will he be in church? Or at the vicarage?'

'Why, child, what would you be wanting with the Reverend Starr at this time of day?' the old woman marvelled.

Joanna locked and unlocked her hands in her agitation. 'I don't want to go in the boat. I don't want to do anything. I just ... want to sit quiet in church,' she finished unaccountably.

Mrs Bird laid a cool hand on Joanna's hot forehead, and Joanna pulled away, stung. 'Don't touch it!' she said fiercely.

'Lor, miss, I'm just seeing if you're feverish,' the old woman soothed.

'Don't touch it! That's what I got, when I was with...'

She bent forward, her arms crossed over her chest, her face agonized, as if consumed with an inner pain that wouldn't ease.

'He's dead, you know. I only just heard. All this time I thought he wasn't dead, but he is.

It's all over. Finished. Ended. Nothing else. Might as well be dead myself.'

Mrs Bird poured some whisky into the bottom of a clean cup, and put it to Joanna's lips.

'Maybe t'would be as well if you did see the Reverend,' the old woman said thoughtfully.

'He was a bit like Mr Starr,' Joanna went on, drinking the whisky, and talking as if driven by something inside her, which gave her no peace. 'He talked to me like Mr Starr does. He made me see what sort of person I was. No one else ever has. Mr Starr is the link. If I keep looking at him, I shall see Bill, and he won't be dead any more, and...'

'Now, miss, that'll do,' Mrs Bird said firmly. 'One thing I am *not* having is wild talk. It will *not* do. Now, some more whisky, and then to bed with you, and I've a great mind to send down to the village for Dr Varley, that I have!'

Dr Varley was out, but the old woman insisted on leaving a message that he was to come up to her cottage as soon as he returned. 'I've put the poor lass in bed with a lacing of whisky and aspirin, but she's not right, by a long chalk, and I can do no more.'

When she came back to the cottage, she found Garry there, fuming because no meal was laid for him, and because Joanna was so sound asleep that he couldn't wake her.

'You leave the poor lass be,' Mrs Bird said angrily. 'You told me, sir, to tuck her up for a nap. You saw how she was!'

'A nap's a nap, but she wanted this show to-night, and it'll be too late soon.'

'She's not moving out of that bed until the doctor comes up,' the old woman said firmly. 'I'd never look the doctor straight in the face again if I was to let that child go out in a boat to-night – *boat*, the idea!'

Garry smiled, and said meekly, 'Well, I suppose you're right, Mrs Bird,' and settled down to wait quietly while she got him something to eat.

After his meal, he wandered outside and stood smoking, and then said he would go up to his room. The old woman was busy at the sink, and paid little attention to him.

He went into Joanna's room and shook her softly, keeping a hand over her mouth in case she made a sound on waking.

Her eyelids lifted heavily, and although he repeated his instructions two or three times over, in simple words and a clear insistent undertone, she looked as if she still didn't understand. Finally, he dragged her out of bed, and thrust her clothes into her hands. As he shut the door, he saw her sway a little, and then begin to sort her day clothes from the bundle he had thrust at her.

He shut the door, and stayed outside,

listening with a fever of impatience. Downstairs, he could see the old woman pottering about, preparing a stew for the next day's meal. A little later, according to her usual habits, she would go outside and pull up a few root vegetables, and some salad lettuce. Her life went by clockwork. She also went round the little house, with the hurricane lantern, making war on the insect pests in the primitive traps she had set.

While she was out at the back Garry got Joanna downstairs and out of the cottage, down the gap and along the beach to the little jetty where he had moored the boat. The tide was up, and it wasn't easy to get Joanna aboard. She moved as if her legs wouldn't work properly, and once in the boat, she subsided and fell fast asleep.

He draped a raincoat over her and made her roughly comfortable. Sooner or later, she would wake with the flying spray on her face, and then would be the time for argument.

They were well out to sea before Joanna stirred. She lay there watching the merging of day and darkness in a superb sky, and then, as Garry shut off the engine, she said, in a clear little voice: 'Bill, are you sure you're not driving too fast?'

Garry watched her, his face a study. He had seen Joanna in many moods, but never quite like this.

Then she saw him, standing silhouetted against the night sky. In the waning light, Garry saw a smile of incredible beauty touch her mouth and creep up to her eyes. She cushioned her head in one arm, and murmured sleepily, 'Bill, even you forget to play safe sometimes!' and she closed her eyes again.

Garry watched her quietly enough, but his face flamed, and turned an ugly purple. Never in his life had he been in such a rage against another man. Most of the women he had known had owed no particular loyalties to anyone, and hadn't lasted long, but while they had lasted, he had enjoyed them. They had been his. Joanna had never been his. Only by telling her that this man was dead, had he any hope. One day some fool would come along and tell her something else, and then his loose hold on her would slip away.

'Joanna! Pull yourself together!' he shouted. 'Get up, girl, and let the wind blow on your face! We're not in a car, we're in the *Seagull*, out in mid-Channel. Can you hear me?'

Her eyes fought themselves open, and she stared uncertainly up at him. He pursued his momentary advantage ruthlessly.

'This is Garry – Garry Wetherall, and we're standing to, and looking for the contact boat from France. Remember? If the going's good, we'll be back. If things turn out wrong, we'll cut and run, maybe to France, maybe to Holland. Can you hear what I'm saying? Do you understand me?'

For a second she stared, a vague expression on her face, and then she struggled up on to her knees, grasping, for her, the essential point.

'Garry!'

'Yes, Garry,' he insisted grinning. 'Garry, remember? You're too full of that old hag's bad whisky. Get up, girl, and feel the wind on your face.'

She got up, and it struck him that she was in the mood to do anything he liked to tell her. How long it would last, he had no idea. He'd just never seen her like this before.

She pulled herself up, and he watched her cautiously. She stood clutching the side, staring with incredulous dark eyes at the faint line of lights that was the shore, and all around them the expanse of darkening sea. She felt little and lost, and because boats and sea and wind and flying spray were mixed up in it, the lost feeling had a strong flavour of the desolation of her childhood, when she had lived in the port, and no one had wanted her except her grandfather. Now he was gone, and Bill was gone...

Her head became clearer, and she swung round on Garry.

'I don't remember how I got here,' she accused.

'I don't suppose you do, honey,' he grinned. 'You were practically out on your feet. I thought you had a better head for spirit.'

'I didn't want to come,' she told him.

'Did you tell them – old mother Bird and that son of hers?' he asked, suddenly remembering something.

'I really can't remember,' she said, with something of her old spirit. 'But you'd better tell me something, Garry. What did you mean about cutting and running? And France and Holland? What have they got to do with a fishing trip?'

He stared at this new mood she had slipped into, after doing as he had invited her, and let the wind whip her face. And then he started to laugh.

'Honey, if you don't know what I'm up to, then you're a bigger mug than even I took you for! Oh, don't worry, if they catch up on us, there's nothing to show for their pains.'

'Then why all this talk of cutting and running!' she retorted. 'Oh, stop looking for any contact boat, Garry. There'll be nothing here to-night. The coastguards are out!'

He swung round on her, his face ugly. 'What was that, Jo?'

'They must be,' she said, thinking. 'That's why Isaac Bird warned me not to come. Then he went.'

'You told them what we were going to do?

Are you such a big fool that I still have to warn you when you have to keep your mouth shut? Why, I only left you to put the car away!'

'And I told them we were going fishing, but they seemed to think we were going to do something else,' she said, starting to laugh.

Almost beside himself with fury, he lifted an arm and struck at her. For ever conscious of the injury to her forehead, she ducked, and caught the blow on her shoulder, reeling against the side. He grabbed her, and steadied her, but the sea had heaved itself up almost to her, in that split second.

'Joanna!' Garry was shouting. 'Joanna, for heaven's sake, think! It's us – we're in this together, kid! What else did you tell them?'

'Nothing! I didn't know anything else. I was a fool, as you said just now. But I'm not any more. You put me back to shore, this minute!'

'Are you out of your mind? Even if I could, I wouldn't – with all you know, and in this mood of yours, why, you'd open your mouth so wide–'

A subdued halloo-ing over the water made him peer eagerly into the fast growing darkness. Lights, in varying size and brightness, were dotted over the water. Their own engine, leaping suddenly into noisy life, drowned the sounds of other craft, and also

Joanna's voice, as she shouted urgently to him.

'It's the contact boat – she's here!' Garry yelled.

'Put me back to shore, Garry!'

'Not on your life!' he shouted, grinning over his shoulder.

'Then I'm going myself!' she roared back at him.

He shut off his engine and put about, unbelieving. The voices were still calling to him, from the other boat, but there was a new sound. A nearby engine. Joanna was nowhere to be seen.

A searchlight beam shot across the water, picking him out. It also picked out a small struggling figure in the sea, between the two vessels. Voices yelled imperatively to him. Panic settled on him for a second. Then making up his mind, he started up his engine again, and put about. Anything, to get out of that searchlight beam.

Enveloped in the surrounding darkness once again, he zig-zagged, trying to find his contact boat, but there was no sign of her. The beam of the searchlight would have warned her, and she had gone. He had told Joanna that they would cut and run, but he hadn't meant in his own small, frail craft. He hadn't enough petrol, anyway. Sweat ran down his face. He must find the contact boat. He couldn't stay in this busy traffic lane all night. He started halloo-ing, in a despairing hope of attracting their attention, but all that came back to him was something which sounded like a faint echo, or perhaps Joanna's voice, crying from the water...

CHAPTER TWELVE

Joanna was ill for a much longer time than she could ever remember. She was taken from the cottage to the local hospital, and from there to a small and expensive nursing home. Here, she was visited again by Charles Lindsay, who spoke gently to her, as if he had known her a very long time, but didn't mind her tricks in the least.

When she was well enough to talk to him, she said faintly: 'I wonder you bother with me.'

'Oh, I don't know, Joanna,' he smiled easily. 'You get under people's skins, you know. You'll laugh, I suppose, but there was a time when I even considered working up a much stronger feeling for you than I have.'

'But you thought better of it,' she said, trying to grin.

'Oh, there's enough trouble in this wicked world, without planning some special trouble for myself,' he smiled.

Always she was haunted by a fear she hadn't been able yet to put into words. One day she managed to voice it.

'Did they put my picture in the newspaper again?'

'Good heavens, no. You were mentioned, of course. Why not? Flinging yourself in the water like that, was heroism, my girl!'

She shook her head weakly, and slow tears rolled out of the corners of her eyes. 'No, funk. Just funk. I couldn't go through with it.'

'If "it" means keeping more or less safe and dry in that motor craft, I think I'd have chosen that way, rather than chucking myself overboard into a sea like that.'

'I didn't think. Anyway, I do swim,' she murmured.

A long time afterwards, she again taxed him about the whole affair. On that occasion, she was allowed to sit up, and was wearing a wonderful bedjacket which Lady Lonsdyke had sent for her.

'She wants you back, Joanna. She loves you, you know,' Dr Lindsay said.

Joanna refuted the idea. 'She started something, and she hates it because I didn't let her finish it. I ought to have done well for myself socially, and then she'd have been happy and felt amply repaid for her kindness. As it was, all I did was to make her feel that there wasn't much in this kindness stunt.'

'Except that with her, it isn't a stunt. It comes from the heart,' he reminded her. 'Won't you let her take you back, Joanna?'

'No. Not after all that happened. What

happened to Garry, or aren't I supposed to know?'

He shrugged. 'No one knows, for certain. At a rough guess, I'd say he ran out of juice, and got run down by a Channel steamer or something. Do you care, Joanna?'

She drew in a sharp breath, and then said: 'No, I don't think so. I ought to, I suppose. He's my kind. But I don't.'

'Joanna,' Dr Lindsay said, leaning forward, and speaking earnestly, 'you've never asked me how I came to find you here.'

'Oh, I expect Lady Lonsdyke ran me to earth, didn't she? I guessed there'd be newspaper publicity. I don't seem to be able to avoid it.'

He smiled faintly, but went on: 'Lady Lonsdyke didn't run you to earth. We've been trying to find you, but kept coming to a dead end. It was one of your new friends who contacted us.'

'New friends?' she asked sharply.

He nodded. 'You told me once that you were quite alone, that you were used to it, and didn't really care. Well, you're not alone any more, my dear. You've made a lot of friends, friends you'll keep, if you're wise. Old Mrs Bird, in the cottage. Her son, the coastguard who fished you out of the water–'

'So it was Isaac,' Joanna broke in. 'I thought he hated me! He seemed to, anyway.'

'And your good friend, the Reverend Arthur Starr.'

She turned sharply away.

'What's the matter, my dear?'

She said sharply: 'I don't want to hear about him. It's all over.'

'What is?'

'I asked him to do something for me, but he didn't, and now it doesn't matter.'

'I know. He told us. He did do it, Joanna. You've got to thank him for many things. You ought to, you know. Won't you see him?'

'No! I've said no, every time someone's asked me. I don't care how often he comes. I don't want to see him any more.'

She closed her eyes, and heard Dr Lindsay go out. Her little room seemed very lonely without the warmth in his voice. She dug her nails into the palms of her hands, and kept her eyes closed. Soon it would be tea-time, and very soon afterwards there would be no more visitors for the day, and she would be safe.

She didn't hear her next visitor come in. Only when a voice said mildly, 'I had to gate-crash, or you'd have said no again!' did she realize that her clergyman friend was there beside her.

'Oh, go away!' she said, her face crumpling.

'When I've delivered my news,' he said, composedly, sitting down on the chair

251

which Dr Lindsay had vacated. 'Mrs Bird sends her love, and a fresh-baked cake. Here it is. I've brought you some late roses from my garden, and a book you once expressed an interest in, and if you're not going to stop crying, I'll have to come back to-morrow, but I'll come!'

She wiped her face savagely, and said: 'I suppose I have to thank you for your efforts, and your gifts, but you're too late with your news. I know about William. I don't know why clergymen always love to tell people about deaths.'

'That's unjust,' he observed, looking steadily at her. 'Besides, you've been misinformed. When I saw your William three days ago–'

'You *saw* him?' she gasped.

'I did,' he told her, 'and I quite liked him. Now, where did you get your news from, child?'

'But Garry said, *Garry* said–'

He waited quietly until her wild crying was over, and then he took her hand and held it while he talked to her.

'It isn't going to be easy, Joanna, child. He's ill. He was very badly hurt in that crash. But you knew that.'

Her eager dark eyes raked his face, and then the light died out of them.

'But he never sent for me,' she whispered. 'He never sent for me.'

Mr Starr's eyes fell at that. Watching him all the time, she said bitterly: 'And then there's Lavinia. You forgot to mention her, didn't you?'

'If Lavinia is the young lady who decided that she didn't want to go on with her engagement plans, when her fiancé was so badly knocked about–' Mr Starr began.

'She didn't go *on?*' Joanna gasped. 'She backed out? Left him? Then why, why–'

'Joanna, you have to believe me, child, when I say that there's a very special reason why he didn't send for you.'

'Oh, his mother,' Joanna said, with relief. 'Yes, he wouldn't want her to know. I forgot.'

'When you're well enough, child, will you go to him?'

'Of course I will,' she said, her eyes glistening. 'But when *will* I be well enough? *When?*'

'You look on the mend already,' he said, with a smile, as he got up to go.

Joanna watched the falling leaves from her window, and chafed against the necessity to lie there. She had suffered, among other things, from exposure in the water, from injury as she left the boat, and from a weakness which had set in afterwards. The loss of the old energy seemed to her to be a permanent thing, and when she first put her feet to the ground again, she had a curious conviction that she would never be well

253

enough to make the journey to Pevensey House, and so she would never see William again.

Everyone wrote to her. Even William's mother, who said she could never forgive herself for all the things that had happened to estrange them all.

'I know, my dear,' she wrote, 'I know only too well that William didn't want to marry anyone of my choice, but the best of mothers make the mistake of thinking that they can see further than their sons. I thought that I could see an unhappy future for both you and my son, if I didn't intervene. And now I have lost my chance to set things back as they were. One cannot turn back the clock, that is a simple truth. But it is only by bitter personal experience that we learn to accept it.'

That part of her letter worried Joanna so much that she read on unseeingly. That Mrs Fenton was inviting her to go and live, actually *live*, with her, at Pevensey House, entirely escaped her. The words were there. Joanna read them. But they didn't make sense.

Sitting by her fire one cold autumn day, still only in her dressing-gown, she watched Dr Lindsay pour tea for her, and the nurse fuss around making her comfortable, before she left them.

'Isn't it a funny thing?' she mused,

absently sipping the hot sweet liquid. 'I've never had a real home, and this room is coming to mean more to me than anywhere else. I think I'm making roots here, Dr Lindsay.'

'Oh, I wouldn't do that,' he said hastily. 'And can't you bring yourself to call me "Charles" without any great strain? After all, whichever family you settle with, either at St Christopher's or Pevensey House, I'm a family friend of both, and I'm not likely to get thrown out at any time. So we shall be seeing quite a lot of each other,' and he smiled engagingly.

'Lady Lonsdyke wants me. Mrs Fenton wants me. Mrs Bird wants me. Mr Starr said his sister'd love to have me, if I ever wanted a home.' She shrugged, almost despairingly. 'It just doesn't make sense. Even you extending the hand of friendship, while not so long ago I was just that awful Joanna person that everyone wanted to see the back of, as quickly as could be arranged. I don't ... understand.'

'It's very simple. You've battened on our exterior walls so that we've had to take the barriers down. Perhaps it might have been as well as if we hadn't taken them all down at once, but allowing for human nature being what it is, and the sheep-like instinct of us all, we meant well.'

'All right. So you all like me. I'm now

persona grata everywhere. I may call you Charles. Well, will you now stop keeping me out of everything, and tell me what this horrible letter from Mrs Fenton means, because I just don't understand it at all. Why is it too late? Why doesn't William write to me?'

Charles Lindsay took the letter and silently read it. 'I would hardly have called it a horrible letter, Joanna,' he said at last, handing it back to her. 'I would have said that every line had heart break in it, my dear. She's been with him all the time. You haven't – you've had no idea. You've had troubles of your own.'

'Well, *tell* me about it. Is he still too ill to write to me?'

'No-o,' Dr Lindsay said.

'Then *why* doesn't he?'

'He isn't able to,' he offered, after a long silence.

'Why? Is his hand injured? He can talk on the telephone, can't he?'

She waited, sick at heart, while the doctor finished his tea, and absently poured more.

'*Please* tell me – what is wrong with him? Is he blind?' she whispered, clapping a hand to her mouth as she whispered the words.

'He isn't blind, my dear, but you must wait till you see him. When you can really get out, one of us will take you down to Pevensey House, and his mother wants to talk to you about him first.'

'It's something horrible, isn't it? Why do you have to be so cruel? Why can't *you* tell me? You know, don't you? Mr Starr knows. He saw him. He said he liked him. What did he say when he got my letter? He did get it, didn't he? You did give it to William for me, didn't you?'

'No, I didn't,' he said unwillingly.

'But *why?*'

'It ... would have spoiled our plans. One day, soon, you'll see that, and understand, and even be glad. Joanna, my dear, there are things you don't realize. I don't know much about your early life, and absolutely nothing about your antecedents. I did try to find out. Lady Lonsdyke asked me to. But there was literally nothing to go on. I couldn't find anyone living who'd known your parents.'

'What's all this got to do with William?'

'Quite a lot,' he said composedly. 'What I'm getting at is, I know you suffered privations after you left Scotland. Then you had almost two years of soft living with Lady Lonsdyke, in warm climates, and came back here to the shock of an accident, and then plunged yourself into that old life again, when your body wasn't attuned to it. You weren't hard any more, Joanna. Your body couldn't take it.'

'You mean ... I'm ill?'

'I mean you're not as tough as you

evidently thought you were, and without knowing family medical history, I simply can't forecast how things will go with you. We none of us can. You must take care of your health for a long, long time. That is why we are all of us urging you, either to go back to Lady Lonsdyke, or to William's mother. Where you'll be taken care of.'

'To William's mother,' she said, at last comprehending what that would mean. 'Then I shall be with him, in the same house.'

Charles Lindsay nodded unhappily. 'Personally I should advise you to go back to Lady Lonsdyke.'

Her eyes met his and the excitement died. 'But you don't say *why*.'

She leaned back, her eyes closing on the slow tears that forced their way through the lids. 'He didn't want to marry Lavinia. He told me so. It was me he loved. He *must* have loved me, or he couldn't have...' she broke off, biting on her lip, as she recalled every sweet second of that scene by the wishing well in the woods. 'We would have been married all this time,' she whispered, half to herself, 'if the crash hadn't come. Did he tell his mother?'

'No,' Charles Lindsay conceded, still in that unwilling tone.

'But he told you? You were his friend.'

'No. He told no one. We guessed.'

She nodded, and he realized unhappily that she was coming to the conclusion in her own mind that William Fenton had regretted the whole thing, and hadn't even asked for her. There was nothing he could do about it, without breaking his word to Mrs Fenton, so he just sat watching her, acutely unhappy for all of his friends, especially Joanna, and unable to stir a finger for any of them.

'Have faith, my dear. Just as soon as you're well enough you shall go and see him, and then you'll know everything.'

It was well after Christmas when Joanna was taken to Lady Lonsdyke's house. While in the nursing home, she had caught a chill, and to her intense irritation, they treated her like a hot-house plant, and kept her in bed. When she recovered from that, at Charles' instigation, she had another operation on her forehead, which finally left her skin smooth and clear again, and as far as she could see, no trace whatever of the scar. She asked no questions, and suffered everything to be done to her in a way that was so un-Joanna-like that Charles was worried. He had had every intention of taking her down to Lady Lonsdyke's home himself, but at the last moment wasn't able to.

Finally, the Reverend Arthur Starr offered to make the journey with her.

'I don't see why you had to bother,' Joanna said faintly, as they helped her down the steps to the Lonsdyke car, with the new chauffeur at the wheel. 'I could have gone by myself.'

'I wanted to, my child,' he said with a smile. 'I love that independence of yours, and I don't want you to lose it, but be good enough to spare me from it. I like to think that we're still friends, you know.'

'If you're my friend,' she said, with a trace of her old fierceness returning, 'then tell me what it's all about. They've made a mystery of it, and they're all going to talk at me, but I don't want any of it. If they hadn't frightened me with all that taking-care stuff, I'd even have—'

'Run away again?' he smiled. 'And what would Bill say to that, I wonder? He struck me as a very straight young man, a type after my own heart. My only sense of wonderment lies in why he didn't run off with you when you first met. According to you, Joanna, my dear, you led him a pretty dance all along!'

'Did he tell you anything about that?' she asked quickly.

He looked at the countryside tearing past, and at the impassive back of the new chauffeur, behind his glass screen. They were alone, he and Joanna, in a tight little world of a few feet square. He had her to himself for perhaps the last time, and he made up his mind on the instant.

'I'm going to tell you, Joanna, all about it,' he said.

She caught her breath, and waited.

'I know these good people, your friends, wanted most particularly to tell you themselves. They wanted to "break" the news gently. I believe it would be better for you to tell you at once. You've got courage. You can take it. Oh, I'm breaking no promise. They merely insisted their instructions. I neither agreed nor disagreed with them.'

'Tell me,' she said piteously. 'You've seen William. Is he – is he–'

'He looks, I imagine, pretty much as he used to. No scars. No injured limbs. Beyond a slight limp, he gets about pretty well. I walked with him the length of the drive, in fact.'

She gasped, her dark eyes enormous. 'Then what–?' she whispered.

'He never mentioned you. You've been told that, I believe. He didn't mention you, nor the accident, nor anything before that date, for the simple reason that he doesn't remember.'

He looked into her eyes.

'Do you understand, my dear? His memory's gone, and so far, nothing can bring it back, unless you can. You, it seems, are the link.'

He was aware that she was shivering.

He left her alone for some time, and then he took her cold little hand in his.

'We have to be thankful for so many things, Joanna. Considering he was so badly injured, he's made a wonderful recovery. Day by day, I understand he's doing more and more. He's cheerful and fit. And perhaps one day, some little thing will start the train of memory working again.'

She brought her eyes round to him, and he was astonished to see stark horror in them.

'It isn't anything to be frightened about, my child. It's just a thing needing patience, and love, and faith. Faith comes, if you have the other two, as I believe you have!'

'You don't understand!' she burst out, with something of the old passion and energy. 'You just don't understand! He loved me, once. But what is love? Is it of the mind? Or the heart? Is it there all the time, to be picked up and dusted and shaken in the air? Will it be rusty? Or will it have withered? How can it be there any longer? If he doesn't remember me, do you think he'll see me and fall flat on his face overcome with love for me? No, that isn't what I want. If he falls in love with someone else. Lavinia, for instance, who may well decide, as you seem to have done, that jettisoning the past isn't such a bad thing for anyone to do. No, I want none of it. I wish I hadn't come. I wouldn't have come, if I'd known before.'

'Then you've no love left for him, child?'

'No love left? What a question! What an unanswerable question,' she cried. 'Of course I have. It hasn't changed. But then I've been in love with him, I think, from the first moment I saw him. Much good it did me. What is it but a driving emotion, a need? Oh, words don't begin to cover it. Antagonism was always there, a desire to quarrel with him, an empty aching when he wasn't there, and irritation when I was with him. And then, sometimes, there'd be peace, when our minds touched on some point or other, and it was so wonderful, I used to pray the moment would never end. But it did, of course. And then where would we be? I was ignorant, I had no words to express my meaning then, and he'd so much in the opposite direction. Sometimes I thought I hated him. I didn't, of course, but you see how complex it all is.'

'I do, indeed,' he said, more to encourage her to go on, than by way of agreement.

'If his mind has gone—'

'I didn't say that!' he burst out, horrified. 'I said his memory had gone. Perhaps "gone" isn't the right word. It isn't functioning. One day, perhaps, it will, but everything is there, lying dormant, ready, I suppose, to be jogged into working order again. But you'll find no difference in him, my child.

It's just that he doesn't recall a thing beyond the time when he recovered consciousness after the crash. A merciful providence provided, I believe, that he should have no recollection of that crash. You were with him, and then he was alone, remember.'

'I had to get help!' she protested, and when she found he only nodded, and said no more on the subject, she let it drop, and as if exhausted by her outburst, sank back into the seat and closed her eyes.

After a little while, he said: 'Well, my dear, we're nearly at our journey's end, and there is more I have to say to you. But first of all, are you sorry I told you, like this?'

'No. No, not sorry. I rail at you, but you've been so good to me. The best friend I have.'

'Then you'll keep in touch with me, and not hesitate to call on my services, if you need help?'

She nodded, her eyes glistening.

'Good. Good. Now, what I suggest is that you go to Pevensey House, and not to Lady Lonsdyke's, to live permanently. Yes, do it, child. It will hurt at first, but better to take the plunge. You can do so much more good there, on the spot.'

'No, no!' she cried. 'How can I see him every day, and know he doesn't know me?'

'It seems that from the very first, he rather wanted you there as his mother's companion. Now it strikes me as rather a good idea that you go there right away in that capacity. He'll get used to you and it'll be a good reason for your being there. That, I think, is essential – you must have some reason, or he'll be uneasy and suspect something's not quite right.'

'What will his mother say to that?'

'She will welcome it, I know.'

'And Lady Lonsdyke?'

'She suggested it. She's a very wise woman.'

'I know. And my natural reaction is to loathe everyone who has good common sense. Why do people want anything to do with me?'

'You grow on us,' he smiled. 'Now, a further piece of advice, Joanna. Learn to drive a car again. Yes, I know, the idea strikes you with horror, but you must. Within the limits of your health, you must conquer that shrinking from the things you used to do. Drive, climb, even ride horses again. You'll be no good to yourself or to that nice young man, if you don't get back your confidence.'

That was in late January. Joanna quietly slid back into the life of Pevensey House, as if there had been no break, with the single exception that she herself was different. She recalled with a smile, how she had shrunk into a corner of the massive dark old library, and had been afraid of the dogs. It hadn't been easy to get over that fear, but recalling

Arthur Starr's words, she had casually strolled in, and over to the big fireplace, and the once-snarling brutes had got up of their own accord, and moved out of her way. And William had been courteous to her, as if she had been a stranger.

That was the worst moment, when she had first met him again.

'This is my new companion, dear,' his mother had said. 'You've been urging me so long to get one, and now I have, just to please you.' She had paused a fraction of a second, before saying, 'Joanna Roberts.' Both Mrs Fenton and Joanna had waited with bated breath, but there had been no reaction. They might just as well have said that her name was Pixie Bellamy, Joanna thought, wildly, for all the notice he took. He seemed pleased to see the newcomer, for his mother's sake, but there the matter ended.

'But I'm just the same!' Joanna choked, after he had quietly gone out of the room.

'No, dear, not the same,' his mother said, putting an arm round her. 'Not the same at all. Yes, I know you've had your hair cropped short again, but that isn't where the difference lies. I know. Remember, I didn't see you when you came back from the world tour. I haven't seen you since you ran away from here, remember? You're not the same person.'

'You mean I've been polished up,' Joanna said bitterly.

'A little,' Mrs Fenton smiled, 'but it goes deeper than that. You've travelled, and you can't do that without gaining a great deal. You've seen more of the world than I have, and at a time when impressions go deepest. You've met so many people, and you know how you react on them. I think perhaps you've grown up. You're not our mad little Joanna any longer.'

'You don't like me any more?' Joanna frowned.

'I like you more than I think I wanted to,' Mrs Fenton said, smiling ruefully.

The winter was a long one that year, but it didn't stop Joanna from doing the things which her old friend had advised her to. She found she didn't fear driving as much as she'd expected, and one day she forced herself to drive to the place where William had left the car that last time, before going through the woods to the well.

It was a snowy day, although it was the beginning of March. There was a keen wind blowing, and twice she lost the way before she stumbled on the gully. Everything looked changed, under its mantle of snow, even the wishing well. This was the thing she had dreaded. All the other places that had meant so much to her, she had made a point of visiting, but this was the last. When it came to the point, she stared at it, and there were no more tears to shed. There was that old emptiness, which she couldn't write off as the effect of the snow altering everything. It would have been just the same if she had waited till the spring before coming to the place.

She stumbled back to the car, and wondered if this was one risk too many, and whether she would get ill through being out so long in the cold. Suddenly it no longer mattered. She saw that she couldn't go through life, being careful, and hoping. This thought was in her mind when she saw William, walking sturdily along about three miles from Pevensey House, stumping his ash stick into the snow, his limp hardly showing at all.

She slowed down, and waited for him. 'Want a lift?' she called.

'No, thanks. Out walking. Got to finish the walk, you know.'

She pulled up. 'I've just been to the Well Woods. Did you know there was an old wishing well still there?' She asked it with brutal bluntness, and watched him.

'There may be,' he said at last. 'Funny day for a trip like that, isn't it?'

'No. I made myself go.'

He looked sharply at her, inquiry in his eyes.

'I think we've all got things at the back of

our mind that we shrink from. Mine's a car crash. The well's all tied up with it. I made myself go and look at it.'

There was a worried look in his eyes, that wasn't new. His mother usually said hastily, when she saw it, 'Don't bother now, dear. It will come back later.' Joanna wondered whether that was the right thing to do. How long had they to wait? How long must William wait?

'What happened?' he breathed.

'I'm not afraid of it any more,' she told him. 'Like I hated the thought of driving again, but now I don't care.'

He nodded, still with that worried look.

'Get in,' she said. 'D'you think I can go back to the warm house and know you're wandering about in the snow?'

The flicker of a smile chased over his face, and without a word, he got in beside her. As far as she knew, it was the first time he had consented to get into a car since the crash.

Without thinking, she said under her breath: 'Good for you, Bill, that's a step forward!'

She drove on without looking at him, and then was aware that his gloved hands were still gripping the top of his ash stick, in a hold that almost made them tremble. As she came within sight of the gates of Pevensey House, he eased his grasp on the stick, and stretched out his long legs, the first movement of the kind since he had got into the car. As if he had no more terror of it.

'You know,' he said ruminating, 'that wanted a bit of doing, you going to face that place this morning. I'll have to do that, when I find myself not wanting to see a place.'

She nodded, and gently eased the car down the hill and round the S-bend at the bottom.

'Joanna,' he said, laughing a little. 'That must be the standard name for strong-minded young women. I remember that we had another Joanna once. She was a protégée of my mother's, too. She ran bull-headed at things...'

He broke off, lost in his own thoughts.

Joanna swung the car round between the stone pillars of the wide open gates, her heart soaring, a great lump in her throat. The gardener, following a new custom, called out to her: 'All right, Miss Roberts?'

And that, too, was all part of this wonderful day, with the snow, and William there beside her, and the things he had said.

'Yes,' she called out. 'I think so. I think it's *going* to be!'

The publishers hope that this book has given you enjoyable reading. Large Print Books are especially designed to be as easy to see and hold as possible. If you wish a complete list of our books please ask at your local library or write directly to:

Dales Large Print Books
Magna House, Long Preston,
Skipton, North Yorkshire.
BD23 4ND

This Large Print Book, for people
who cannot read normal print,
is published under the auspices of

THE ULVERSCROFT FOUNDATION

... we hope you have enjoyed this book.
Please think for a moment about those
who have worse eyesight than you ...
and are unable to even read or enjoy
Large Print without great difficulty.

You can help them by sending a
donation, large or small, to:

**The Ulverscroft Foundation,
1, The Green, Bradgate Road,
Anstey, Leicestershire, LE7 7FU,
England.**
or request a copy of our brochure for
more details.

The Foundation will use all donations
to assist those people who are visually
impaired and need special attention
with medical research, diagnosis
and treatment.

Thank you very much for your help.